My Precious Sunbeam

By Valerie Baxter

Strategic Book Publishing and Rights Co.

Copyright © 2017 Valerie Baxter. All rights reserved.

No part of this book may be reproduced or transmitted in any form or by any means, graphic, electronic, or mechanical, including photocopying, recording, taping, or by any information storage retrieval system, without the permission, in writing, of the publisher. For more information, send an email to support@sbpra.net, Attention: Subsidiary Rights.

Strategic Book Publishing and Rights Co., LLC
USA | Singapore
www.sbpra.com

For information about special discounts for bulk purchases, please contact Strategic Book Publishing and Rights Co., LLC. Special Sales, at bookorder@sbpra.net.

ISBN: 978-1-68181-773-6

This book is dedicated to my husband, daughters, and granddaughters, and to the memory of our late daughter, Sue, who was killed when the plane carrying the Iowa State University track team crashed returning from a meet in Wisconsin.

PART I

My name is Alice, probably not the right name for a girl who turned out to be such a tomboy. I was born at the beginning of World War II and brought up and nurtured by my wonderful maternal grandparents, Edith and Charles Martin. They must have had the patience of saints as I continually thought of dastardly deeds to amuse myself, but as far as my Nan was concerned, I could do no wrong, even though some of my so-called jokes were aimed at her. I actually thought I was hilarious, as most tricksters do.

They initially hailed from the Isle of Wight, a small island off the coast of Southern England, but moved to Gravesend, Kent, when Grampy's company moved to Tilbury in Essex, a large port at that time. He worked as one of the Chief Engineers in the dry docks where work was carried out on the large liners that sailed with a great number of families leaving to start a new life in Australia.

Tilbury was known for being the first port to receive the first West Indian immigrants who landed there on a ship called *Windrush* on June 22, 1948. There were 492 passengers, including one stowaway.

The *Mayflower* carrying the Pilgrim Fathers docked at Gravesend on her way to the Americas, and the American Indian princess Pocahontas is buried there, possibly in the Chapel of Unity. She became a Christian and married tobacco planter John Rolfe and bore him one son, Thomas. Her descendants through her son include First Ladies Edith Wilson and Nancy Reagan as well as astronomer Percival Lovell. It is alleged that Pocahontas died at the age of fifteen.

I don't remember much of the war besides the drone of the doodlebugs and one particular memory of a neighbour coming up the garden path with her torch alight during an air raid. "Put that light out, you stupid woman!" shouted Grampy Martin. He was an air-raid warden and very diligent in carrying out his duties.

One time I hid Grampy's false teeth and forgot where I hid the jar. Luckily, he found it in time to put his teeth in and go to work.

I remember the post-war rationing such as the blue bags to collect our weekly sugar ration, the large block of butter on the counter at the grocer's, who would cut our quota for the week, and the tins of dried egg. All these items were rationed, and when we made our purchases, the grocer cut the little coupons from our family's ration book. We also had small bottles of what was supposed to be concentrated orange juice but was vile.

Friday night was bath night when the tin bath was brought into the kitchen and buckets of water heated on the gas cooker. I went first and then more water was added for Nan and then Gramp. It was also the night of the dreaded syrup of figs!

I was brought up in the Salvation Army. Grampy Martin was in the band, and Nan was in the Songsters. I can see Grampy Martin's cheeks puffing out the *oompah-pahs* on his E-flat bass. I loved the happy singing and the rousing marches.

After the war was over, at the age of six, I joined the Sunbeams. Unfortunately, I was not a good Sunbeam, because I had a rather devilish streak. I doctored the tea with salt, pinched Nan's rock cakes when she wasn't looking, and giggled during prayer time for absolutely no reason. Hiding the music sheets from the Songsters' was another of my transgressions.

Grampy loved his garden and grew all the vegetables and salad produce from seeds that were available at that time. When I was twelve, my cousin Jack came to live with us. Poor Nan, each of us was as bad as the other.

Grampy always walked around the garden when he got home from work. This particular evening, he noticed that an apple was missing from the tree. He called Jack and me over and told us of the disappearance of the apple. Angelically, we both denied any knowledge of its disappearance. (I wonder who ate it!) We saw him give Nan a little grin as he started to go back into the house.

The house only had electricity downstairs and no internal plumbing, save for a cold tap in the scullery. Jack and I used to wind each other up regularly about red Indians. This was initiated by the serial program on the radio about building railways across the United States. Sometimes we were too scared to go up to our bedrooms, and either Nan or Gramp had to accompany us upstairs and tuck us in the feather beds. Even so, we still tried to frighten each other by making strange wailing noises, and it worked; we always ended up frightening ourselves. Eventually even our saintly grandparents at times had enough of our nonsense and shouted up the stairs to settle down "or else."

At the back of the garden was a disused chalk pit that seemed very deep to our eyes. This was a wonderful playground for Jack and me. We constructed a sort of sledge out of one of the old bedframes from the air-raid shelter and used this to fly down the steep sides of the quarry—absolutely fabulous. Inevitably, the obvious happened, and we came a cropper—neither of us had more than bruises, and I had a bloody nose. Jack said, as we hauled the sledge to the top, "If you lie on it, I will pull you along and tell Nan that you're dead." This we did. Jack started calling, and Nan came running out. "What's happened?" she exclaimed."

"She's dead," said Jack gravely. Unfortunately, or luckily for Nan, who was in a dreadful state, I started to giggle and, needless to say, we both received a clump around the ears!

I think that is enough now of my very young years. Jack went back to live with his parents in Twickenham, Middlesex.

PART 2

When I was fifteen, I had my first Salvation Army uniform. I felt so proud walking along the street with my smart uniform, bonnet, and beautiful black-silk stockings with a seam up the back and spotless white cotton gloves. My friend Amy and I started going pub booming, selling *The War Cry* and the *Young Soldier* around the local public houses. We would also sing a hymn if requested by the people in the public house. It probably seems strange to a layman that we should sell *The War Cry* in public houses when we had made a promise not to drink alcohol, but it was the Salvation Army's way of reaching out to those with whom we had no other means of contact.

After the main service on Sundays, all the young soldiers went out into the street to encourage youths (boys and girls) to come and join us for what was known as a Windup. This was a jolly service with some of the bandsmen and the officers playing guitars while we sang songs set to popular music. This was great fun, and most of those we had encouraged to attend behaved well.

I began a romantic relationship with a bandsman named Carl Parry, and I hoped we would marry and go into training together to become Army Officers. However, he moved away to start a new job and did not keep in contact after a while; rumour had it he had met somebody else. Whether or not this was true, I was too proud to find out.

Now aged nineteen, I took a position in Harley Street as personal assistant to a Consultant Obstetrician and Gynaecologist, and I decided to move to London.

I got a small flat on Primrose Hill and got on with my life. Obviously, Nan and Gramp were sad to see me go but thought I was doing the right thing. To their regret, I did not continue attending the Salvation Army services, apart from a few visits to the Chalk Farm Citadel, near my home on Primrose Hill.

My beloved Nan passed away the same year. I was heartbroken, and Gramp never got over his loss.

There was a girl called Carol in the same building working for another Consultant. We became close friends and started to go out for meals, to the pictures, and to the Marquee to see Chris Barber and Ottily Patterson, my favourite trad jazz band. One night we went to the Café de Paris, and I had my first alcoholic drink, a Baby Cham. My first sin!

William Booth, the founder of the Salvation Army, preached against alcohol and the terrible effects it caused in families when the menfolk spent their earnings on drink leaving their families to starve.

Carol and I enjoyed one another's company, and we quite often went to the Café de Paris. On one particular evening, we were sitting having a coffee when a rather suave, good-looking young man came up and asked if he could join us. We both agreed, but during the course of the evening, it was obvious to both Carol and me that he was interested in me. A short while later, Carol and I decided to go home. The young man's name was Patrick, and he definitely did not want to be called Pat. He asked if I would like to have dinner with him. I agreed, and we made a date for two days later—he would pick me up from my home at 7.00 p.m.

I was rather flattered and really looked forward to seeing him again. I asked Carol what I should wear, and she said it should be something conservative. I decided on a grey slim-line dress edged with white that discreetly showed off my neat, shapely body.

Patrick was late arriving, full of apologies, stating that it could not be avoided. We started a light-hearted conversation about holidays and shows we had seen. He asked me where I worked and for whom. Patrick stated that he worked for the Government and was presently attached to the British Embassy. I was rather impressed, being rather naïve.

When we finished our meal and coffee, Patrick asked if he could walk me home, as it was such a beautiful evening and he had not been to Primrose Hill for some considerable time. I agreed, and we set off at a leisurely pace, chatting about anything and everything. After a while, Patrick took my hand; the pit of my stomach flipped, and I felt warm all over. I was rather worried about getting home, as I had been brought up to believe that sexual relations only occurred once you married, and I knew that a kiss could lead to more.

When we walked up the path on Primrose Hill, Patrick turned, put his arms around me and kissed me with such intensity that I virtually swooned. I had never felt such a wonderful feeling before. I tried to explain my moral views to him but was lost for words. How he made head or tails of what I was trying to explain to him, I just don't know, but he did. He left me weak and dying to see him again, which was to be in three days' time.

I had not deserted Carol and, in fact, she too had met someone. When I saw her the following day at work, I explained what had happened and the way I felt. Carol was rather blasé about it, being more experienced than I in matters of the heart.

When we met three days later, Patrick asked me if I was happy in my job. I asked him why, and he said that a job had come up for a PA/Secretary in the British Embassy in Worvocki Street, Budapest, Hungary, and that he was going to be transferred there shortly. I said I would have to think about it very seriously. Patrick said that I would have to take the Civil Service examination, which would give me time to make up my mind. Patrick and I kept in touch regularly.

Of course, there had been the uprising in 1956, when Hungary was invaded by the Russians, which began on 23 October and lasted until 10 November. This was the first major threat to the USSR's forces since they had driven the Nazis out at the end of the Second World War.

I passed my Civil Service exam a couple of months later and had an interview and signed the Official Secret Act, and, at the age of twenty and on 1 October 1960, I was on my way to Budapest. Patrick, or rather Mr. Donnelly, met me at the airport. Apart from a slight peck on both my cheeks, Patrick did not show any great pleasure at my arrival.

It was rather daunting and a little intimidating to say the least. There was an underlying sinister atmosphere, and the Soviets were distinctly unfriendly and austere. As we walked to the car, Patrick explained a little about the spontaneous nationwide revolt against the government of the Hungarian People's Republic and its Soviet-imposed policies. Public discussion of the revolt was suppressed at this time amongst the Hungarians.

I told Patrick how impressed I was with his knowledge, and he stated that it was all part of the job. "Speaking of it all being part of the job," he added, "I'm afraid we've dropped you into the deep end. There is a small reception at the Embassy tonight, nobody of importance will be attending, but we need someone to be there to make sure they are all fed and watered until the Ambassador shows his face. Think you can manage that?" Before I could answer, he added nonchalantly, "I will be there, of course."

Thinking him a little rude, I said I was sure I would have sufficient nous to be able to cope.

We turned into a pleasant tree-lined street and stopped outside a small block of flats. The outside showed evidence of bullet holes, but all in all, it was a pleasant if tired-looking building.

"I am afraid it is the top floor, but there is a lift," said Patrick, but I decided there and then that I would not be using the lift on my own, as it rattled and creaked all the way to the top floor. (Actually, it was only the fourth floor, a comparatively short block for the area.)

Patrick helped me into what appeared to be a rather pleasant, if small, apartment, but made no attempt to kiss me as I was expecting. "I will pick you up at five-thirty and show you the way to the Embassy," he said, all business like and quite off-hand. "It is quite close and straight forward from here."

He turned and ran down the stairs without a backward glance but arrived on time to collect me. I knew I looked good, but Patrick made no comment. We strolled leisurely along the road, and after a short while, he took my hand. Again, my stomach flipped, and I flushed quite obviously.

True to his word, the Embassy was within two blocks, and I made a note of various landmarks that would guide me there the following morning.

The small reception went without a hitch, and when the Ambassador eventually made his appearance, he said, "You must be Alice. Welcome to the Embassy."

"Thank you, Sir," I answered.

"I believe Mr Donnelly is seeing you home this evening."

"I think he is," I replied.

As Patrick and I started our fairly short walk, it began to drizzle, and we used the cover of the many trees as a substitute umbrella. Halfway down the street, Patrick pulled me to him and kissed me with such intensity and obvious longing, just as he had before. We continued to embrace and kiss passionately for so long my lips felt numb.

When we reached my building, the inevitable happened.

"Can I come up?" Patrick said breathlessly and obviously aroused.

"I don't think that would be wise," I said with sincerity. "I have the same urge to make love as you, but you know my view on sex before marriage. I'm really sorry, truly."

Patrick left disgruntled and did not look back.

Once inside the entrance hall of the flats, I decided that I would have to risk the lift, as there were no lights in the stairwells. The only light was the one in the entrance hall.

I found the atmosphere in Budapest tangibly tense since arriving, despite Patrick's reassurances, and I felt quite disconcerted, even though I had only been there a short time. However, I slept well that night and was up bright and early. I showered and dressed suitably for work. I had a coffee from the jar left in the apartment (black, as I had not had the foresight to get any provisions), and I walked leisurely to the Embassy.

When I arrived, I was met by the senior P.A., Janet Smith, who seemed very pleasant. With a warm smile she thanked me for standing in for her the previous night and said that I had impressed the Ambassador and the other staff with my efficient and pleasant manner.

The day flew by, as everyone was very busy. I did not see Patrick at all, and I asked Janet where I could get some provisions. She said that if I could hang on, she could give me sufficient basics to tide me over until either she or someone else could show me where to shop.

I mentioned to her that I felt someone had been in my flat, and I had noticed the smell of cologne.

Janet assured me that this was standard procedure. "A member of our staff, the caretaker, sometimes does a security check on all our premises to make sure all is as it should be," she said. "He was probably checking the flat because you are a new arrival."

True to her word, just as I was about to leave for the day, Janet arrived in my office with milk, butter, bread, a selection of smoked meats and some fruit. I settled up with her and made my way home, feeling pretty weary after a very busy day.

I got into the routine remarkably quickly and struck up a friendship with Janet. We did a little sightseeing. The River Danube was lovely. Of course, at one time Buda was originally a town on one side of the Danube and Pest on the other side, but they were united in 1872 and became Budapest.

There was a Roman church built in the thirteenth century and a seventeenth century basilica, both damaged by the Soviets in World War II and the uprising in 1956. Whilst we were wandering the narrow, cobbled streets looking at the pretty houses with their colourful flower boxes, I thought I saw Patrick ahead going into one of the houses. I did not say anything to Janet.

Late one night, Patrick arrived at my flat very agitated and pale. "Will you post a letter for me, Alice?" he asked.

"Of course," I said. "I have one to post to Grampy anyway."

"Thanks, Alice," he said, and left immediately. I was cross that he seemed to be just using me and was not actually romantically interested in me at all. I now began to wonder why he had asked me to work at the Embassy.

I glanced at the envelope and saw that it was addressed to someone in Russia.

I wrote to Carol and told her that I had blown it with Patrick. I had received a letter from her the previous day telling me she was getting married to Ian and wanted me to be her bridesmaid. I was really happy to be her bridesmaid, and our future correspondence was all about the wedding, what my dress was like, and how happy she was.

It was a June wedding, and I had taken leave to attend it, which the Embassy granted, as I had not taken leave since my arrival in Budapest. I wanted to see Grampy whilst in England, too.

Carol looked beautiful and deliriously happy on her wedding day. I had kept my flat, and when I got back from visiting Grampy in

Gravesend, there was a telegram from Janet Smith telling me that Patrick had been murdered.

Janet asked if I could return as soon as possible as all of Patrick's friends, colleagues, and acquaintances had to be interviewed. Janet said a ticket would be waiting for me at Heathrow the next day for the midday flight, and I was to go straight to the Embassy on my arrival.

I felt a mixture of emotions—sadness, worry and apprehension. I hardly slept that night but didn't cry. I was not in love with Patrick, I was just in love with the feelings he aroused in me.

I arrived at Heathrow looking tired and wan. The flight was on time, and I arrived at the Embassy about four hours later. Janet met me in the main reception with a grim look on her face.

"What on earth has happened to Patrick?" I asked. "Has anyone any clue why he has been murdered?"

"I think it best if we do not discuss this terrible waste of such a young life," Janet said in such a way that I was left with no doubt that this was a taboo subject.

I wondered if anyone knew about my acquaintance with Patrick.

We hung around in our offices, all in sombre mood. Janet came in to say that because Patrick had been murdered outside Embassy property, the Soviet and Hungarian authorities would be involved in the investigation. One by one, the interviews took place, and it was late in the evening when my turn came.

I was first asked about how I had met Patrick and then about our relationship. I told them that since I arrived in Budapest, apart from the one evening he kissed me, we'd had no relationship at all. I was asked if he or any of his friends had been inside my flat. I stated that apart from helping me with my luggage on my arrival, neither he nor his friends had been inside my flat that I was aware of. I also stated that I had not met any of his friends. I never mentioned his late night visit or the fact that I had posted a letter for him. I told them that I had smelled cologne in my flat one time, but nobody seemed to take the slightest interest. They asked if I had visited the main town with Patrick, and I told them I had not. I was told to leave and go home, which I did.

When I let myself in, there was the same smell of cologne, and the flat had definitely been searched. I ran back to the Embassy to tell Janet, who explained that everyone's residence had to be searched upon a request from the Hungarian Government.

After a few weeks of hard work and a strained atmosphere, the Ambassador asked that we assemble in the Committee Room. He told us that all the investigations into Patrick's murder appeared to prove categorically that Patrick had been caught attending an underground meeting of the anti-Soviet faction. Whether he did so as part of his job was not mentioned, nor would it be.

I had been unable to settle since Patrick's death, and I asked if there was any chance of a transfer. Janet said she would look into it and let me know.

I continued working hard to help keep my mind occupied. I obviously had no idea at all about Patrick, and, thinking about it logically, I wondered why he had asked me to come to Hungary and whether there was any sinister motive. I was probably letting my mind run away with wild thoughts, but he certainly had to have picked me out for some reason—definitely not for love though.

Janet and I continued to get out and about as much as possible, and she made several enquiries about a transfer for me to another Embassy, but there were no vacancies at present.

We had a double blind-date one evening, which lasted about thirty minutes and left both Janet and me in stitches, as both dates were incredibly boring and definitely lacking in the "good looks" department.

We visited museums, art galleries and other places of interest, and we became quite close friends.

PART 3

Grampy Martin was attacked in his garden and received a bad blow to his head. I flew home, and he was delighted to see me. He looked very frail.

Apparently, he had caught some youths pinching his precious apples, and things got heated. I think he thought he could teach them a lesson, as he had quite a short fuse. He could not remember much but went to his neighbour's house who, because of Grampy's bad head wound, called an ambulance. He required several stitches.

After this incident, he gradually went downhill and died at the beginning of September 1962 at the age of ninety-six. I was twenty-two.

After Grampy's funeral, I felt the need to go to the Salvation Army. I was so moved by the boundless feeling of love reverberating around the congregation and realised how much I had missed the Army. I felt as if I was walking on air as I returned to my flat. I decided there and then that I would give my notice when I returned to Budapest and try to get into The International Training College of the Salvation Army to become a serving Salvation Army Officer.

Having worked out my notice, I returned to my home in Primrose Hill, London. Janet was rather sad to see me go and surprised at my decision to become a Salvation Army Officer.

I contacted the Officer at Gravesend Corps and asked if he would give me a reference, which he was happy to do. I was interviewed and accepted for training, which involved an in-depth understanding of the Holy Bible, how to prepare and deliver sermons, and how to cope and care for the most vulnerable in society. My two years' training flew by, and the next thing I knew, I was getting ready for my passing-out parade.

During my two years at Training College, Carol and Ian had twins, Christopher and Isobel, born in early 1963. They were adorable, and I would go and see them as often as I could.

I had been allocated a little Corps in the East End, and I was also assigned to help at the William Booth short-term hostel for the homeless, located opposite The London Hospital Whitechapel.

My first meeting, 2 October 1964, went well, although there was only a very small congregation and a band containing only eight musicians, but they were excellent. They were teaching several children from the Sunday School to play various instruments. We had an open-air meeting and marched back to the Hall with the flag flying with me walking beside it in front of the band. My heart swelled.

The next day, I went to do my stint at William Booth House. When I arrived, I was greeted by a Soldier who said she would get Captain Parry. When Captain Parry came to greet me, I could not believe my eyes—it was Carl! Six months later, on 31 March 1965, we stood in front of the altar at my little Corps, with Colonel Les Martin, my uncle, pledging our vows to each other in the presence of God. I am sure Nan and Grampy Martin were looking down on us.

Both Carl and I had to finish our postings, but we were close enough to see each other regularly and spend nights together.

Carl often gave sermons at my Corps, and I started a Sunday School, which turned out to be very successful. I decided to take the children to Southend on Sea as a treat. We were going to have to charge 6d for those who could actually afford it, but one of the senior soldiers at my Corps generously offered to make up the shortfall and pay for anyone who could not afford their own 6d. It was a marvellous day. All the children had a wonderful time and got some fresh air. Most of them fell asleep on the journey home, proof enough of their energetic day. They had been delighted with their bag of chips and batter pieces, probably the last meal they would have until late tomorrow.

I wanted to start a Sunbeam Group, so I wrote to the larger Corps asking if they had any outgrown Sunbeam uniforms to spare. I was amazed at the response, but I had to get the permission of all the parents of those concerned for them to join the Sunbeams and to wear the uniform. Nobody refused. (The Sunbeams were the equivalent to the Brownies in the Church of England.)

Kitty, the Corps Sergeant Major, was a dab hand at needlework, and, after we washed and ironed the uniforms, she set about making them fit all the little girls who wanted to become a Sunbeam.

Carl and I also started a Youth Club, as there was nothing for the young people to do in the area, and many were from poor families. We were amazed at how successful it was, perhaps helped by the biscuits and juice. A local club gave us an old table tennis table and bats, which were greatly used and enjoyed.

Our first task when we started the Sunbeam troop was to teach the little girls the Sunbeams' song.

> A Sunbeam, a Sunbeam,
>
> Jesus wants me for a Sunbeam
>
> A Sunbeam, a Sunbeam
>
> I'll shine for Him every day

It was beautiful seeing these dear children, mainly with grubby faces, singing away. One such child was Maggie, a very thin and neglected little girl of six. I had heard that she was never seen without her uniform on.

Our first badge was going to be sewing, and Kitty was going to help them make a nice handkerchief for their mums. We were fortunate enough to have scraps of material donated by a local draper. When I went to look at how they were getting on, I put my arm across Maggie's shoulders, and she winched. I noticed some bruising on her arms and her lower neck. I discussed this with Kitty and Carl, and we decided to speak to Social Services. It turned out that Maggie's family was already known to them.

Maggie did not appear for a couple of weeks but turned up on the third Monday for Sunbeams.

"Where have you been, Maggie?" I said, giving her a warm smile. "We have missed you."

"I had to look after the baby. Me mum's been ill. Me dad's gone, and I hope he does not come back."

I went to visit Maggie's Mum, who looked worn out. "Are you feeling better now?" I enquired. "Maggie told me you have been ill."

"I'm fine now—my husband has gone and hopefully won't come back. He was very cruel. Maggie has been looking after me well—bringing me milk, fruit and even an occasional piece of meat."

I had heard rumours that a rather scruffy Sunbeam had been helping herself to the odd piece of fruit from the fruit stalls in the market and a bottle of milk from the milk float when the milkman was not in sight. I hadn't heard where she got the meat from, however. I talked to the children at the Sunday School and told them that stealing was a sin. This fell on deaf ears as far as Maggie was concerned, as I soon learned that she was helping several more people who were in need.

I think the tradesmen had rather a soft spot for this increasingly scruffier Sunbeam, and turned a blind eye.

I really loved this dear scruffy little girl.

PART 4

In May 1967, our Division Commander came to see us to ask if we would go to Southern Sudan, as the Officer there had left.

He did not tell us who the Officer was or why he had left.

We said that we would think about it and let him know as soon as we came to a decision. Of course, this was not a hard decision to make, as it was obvious that we were needed in Maroon. We notified our Division Commander the following day that we would both be happy to go to the Sudan.

Carl and I had to attend the Hospital for Tropical Diseases for all our inoculations, which took about six weeks, as some inoculations were in rounds of three injections, one every two weeks.

We were also told the precautions to take against the HIV virus, something we knew nothing about.

We told our soldiers at our Corps, all of whom were sorry we were leaving—the worst of all being Maggie, who sobbed her little heart out. We promised to keep in touch with her and explained that we had been chosen to do God's work in Sudan.

Carol was beside herself and tried desperately to change our minds, but of course she couldn't, and we promised to take care and contact them frequently.

We left the East End in July 1967, and another young couple took our place.

Valerie Baxter

We arrived at the Mission in Maroon, Sudan, tired but happy on 31 July 1967. There was a four-bedroom house for all the staff to occupy. There was a small but pristine little hospital, completely tiled in quality white tiles. The equipment was good. All of this was donated by a most generous benefactor who had remained anonymous.

There was a borehole and a school, which consisted of several brick-built pillars upon which was fitted a corrugated roof to let the air circulate. The Army Hall was small but well decorated. There were three volunteers: Sally Abbot, a retired General Practitioner; Miriam Anzoola, a qualified nurse from the Sudan; and Harry Brown, who looked after the general maintenance of the Mission.

The truck that brought us to the Mission also brought many supplies, including anti-malarial and HIV drugs. Unfortunately, there were no mosquito nets, much to the disappointment of the medical staff.

There was also a newly qualified doctor on his gap year and Brian Cox's replacement. He was due to arrive in the truck bringing much needed vaccines, medicines, saline drips and dressing. The same truck would return Brian, the out-going resident doctor, to Juba, the capital of Sudan, on route for his return home to England.

After we had all introduced ourselves, packed away the few clothes we had other than our tropical uniforms, we sat around the table with a mug of tea and learned about the general running of the clinic. Carl was a qualified teacher by this point and really looking forward to starting up the school again as soon as he could.

As we were sitting there, we heard a great commotion outside. Sally and Miriam dashed out to find several of the villagers, one of whom was carrying an obviously sick child. Sally led the way to the clinic and went in with Miriam and the mother and child. The rest were told to stay outside. It transpired that the child had malaria and was critically ill.

First thing in the morning, Carl and I went to the clinic. Sally was sitting with the broken-hearted mother and a little covered body lying on the bed.

"If only we had more nets, this might not have happened," said Sally wearily. "Sadly, your first service will be a funeral."

Carl conducted the funeral later in the day with such tenderness and compassion that even Harry had a tear in his eye.

Immediately after the funeral service, the truck arrived with the hospital supplies and our own basic food necessities. The truck also brought our new doctor, James Wilson. Sally showed him around the Mission and explained that there was a clinic for inoculations for measles, mumps and German measles later the same day if the parents could be persuaded to come. We were glad to see that twelve families turned up.

There were dressings to be done for ulcers, burns and wounds, which were common, because the people worked their barren land with very crude tools.

I wrote to Carol that evening to say we had arrived safely and how sad we were to have to carry out a funeral on a little child who had died from malaria when a few pounds spent on a mosquito net might have saved his life.

When we sat around the table having supper that evening, James asked us, "How can you believe in God when there is such suffering all around us?"

Carl answered, "A lot of problems are caused by mankind's greed, and if more people helped and thought about the needs of others, much more could be done to alleviate the suffering."

"A baby has just died! One of the millions who dies each year," James retorted. "I just can't equate this to an all-seeing, loving God."

"We can't always understand why things happen, but we must do our level best to help all those in need, whatever that need might be," answered Carl.

"Most people believe that, but they don't believe in God," replied James.

"I will have to try my best to convince you," Carl said amiably.

The following day we were all up with the lark. Harry was getting water for our morning cuppa, and as he did so, a malnourished little girl came with a plastic container to get water for her family. How she managed to lift it was beyond me, but she struggled off with a smile on her tiny face.

"Do many people come for water, Harry?" I asked.

"Yes, some of them walk miles, just like the last little one, but at least they get clean water to drink. It is important that we do not leave any standing water though, as the mosquitos will lay their eggs in it." Harry was a remarkable man. He had made a sewage system of sorts, which was remarkably efficient and hygienic, but only for the use of the Mission. He told us that when there was some spare cash, he wanted to teach each little village how to do the same.

Gradually, during the day, more mothers came with their babies, mainly due to Miriam who had been out and about the villages persuading them of the necessity of the inoculations.

Carl was taking his first class, and the children of all ages were eager and quick to learn. It was incredible how much English they already knew. They poured over the few tatty textbooks that we had, and I was determined to write to my old school asking if they had any spare disused textbooks they could send us, especially those in the subjects of science, physics, maths and English. I stated in my letter that we would be grateful for any books whatever the condition.

That night, the first baby born since our arrival was delivered. The mother had walked a couple of miles to get to the clinic, but she was safely delivered of a baby boy. A poor old man had fallen and landed partly on his fire, and he was brought in with severe burns to his chest. He must have been in agony, but these people were great stoics. Sally, James and Miriam went about the treatment of all their patients most efficiently.

When we met for supper that evening, Harry came out with the worrying news that a very dangerous group of militia had been prowling the area. They were known to carry out widespread human rights violations, including mutilation, torture, slavery, rape, abducting civilians, using child soldiers, using young children as sex slaves and a number of massacres.

"Apparently one village about twenty kilometres away had been attacked. They mutilated several of the older women, hacked to death some of those who could not run away and hide, and took young boys away with them. Some young boys already with them had been made to hack people to death."

"All in the name of their own particular religion, I have no doubt," James said heatedly.

"They are saying that some of the villagers have already left to go to a refugees' camp miles away, and, by doing so, they are putting themselves more at risk," Harry added, ignoring the remark.

"We must have a meeting with the elders of the nearest villages and offer them refuge here, as little as it is," Carl said.

"We must do this tomorrow. There is no time to lose," Harry answered forcefully.

"I will stay in the clinic tonight," said Sally.

To which I replied, "I will stay with you so that James and Miriam are well-rested for tomorrow's clinics."

"I will keep you company," Carl said.

We held a service for the local children to help them cope with their fear. After we told them some stories about Jesus and said a prayer, we gave them each a biscuit and a small orange juice, and they happily went on their way. "See you tomorrow at school," said a little boy with huge brown eyes. "Yes, see you tomorrow," said Carl. All of us wondered if we would see some of those children again.

The elders of some of the villages close by informed us that Government troops were in the area, and hoped they would protect them.

We offered them and all of their people refuge in the compound, but, apart from our converts, no other locals came to us for refuge.

Sally was just coming back from dressing the burns of Jacob, the elderly gentleman, when a truck full of armed, uniformed men came roaring into the compound.

"Can I help you?" Sally asked rather carefully.

A huge black man wearing many braids jumped from the truck. "We are Government soldiers. We are checking on all the missionaries in this area. We are experiencing a very dangerous and volatile situation. The Militia are not far away, and we are not able to safeguard all Missions." He spoke extremely good English and was probably educated in the UK. "I think you should leave as soon as possible," he added.

"That is not an option, as we have patients and refugees here," James said calmly.

"We will do what we can if we are in the area should you come under attack," the soldier told us.

"Thank you," Carl said.

"We are going to fill our water containers from your well and then we will be off." Two soldiers got down from their truck and filled containers with copious amounts of water. Although we had a bore hole, water was a very precious commodity, but obviously none of us wanted to stop them, as they were very intimidating.

My Precious Sunbeam

A couple of days went by and Sally, Miriam and James were busy as usual. As they came for a break, I asked them, "How are the patients today?"

Sally looked very tired. "Three of the children with measles are very poorly with pneumonia. I fear two of them are not going to make it. Miriam will be staying with them tonight."

"I will stay with Miriam," I said, and Carl volunteered to spend the night in the clinic with us.

The following day one of the Medecins Sans Frontier's trucks arrived to make sure we knew the current situation. They were on their way to the nearest refugee camp, about twenty miles away, loaded with medicines, operating equipment and basic provisions. They did, however, have a guard with them.

Unfortunately, they had come across a village decimated by the marauding militia, which had hacked people to death, raped young girls and burnt the village and anyone left in it.

The group of volunteers left. They were such brave people.

James was shattered at this news of the marauding militia, as he had carried out a number of surgical procedures, due to the terrible injuries caused by them. He was giving the anaesthesia himself as well as performing the operations with Sally's help—a very difficult and dangerous thing to do, but he had no alternative, as there was no resident anaesthetist.

On August 22, a truck arrived from Juba with more supplies and several huge parcels, one of which contained numerous textbooks from my old school. There were also some battered musical instruments, including a trombone, a euphonium and a cornet. Harry was delighted. "It will occupy the young ones and hopefully keep their minds off the situation," he said.

There was a letter and a huge parcel from Carol and Ian. In her letter, Carol urged us to come home.

The parcel contained mosquito nets, antibiotics, anti-malarial drugs, treatment for diarrhoea and surgical dressings. Where on earth she and Ian got them is anybody's guess.

Harry and Carl taught some of the children to play the instruments and they loved it. After a short while, they persuaded us to let them play the hymn they had learned. They did their best, but it was excruciating. We all sang as loudly as possible to drown them out and tried desperately not to laugh.

As Sally and James came out from the clinic, they both said in unison, "What on earth was that?"

"That, my dears, was our band," I said jovially.

While we were having supper, we heard the noise of a truck approaching followed by shouting, screaming and the sound of running.

We all dashed outside to find a small group of militiamen, one carrying a badly injured comrade. They grabbed Sally, who had a white coat on, and virtually dragged her across the ground in the direction of the clinic. James and Carl followed but were both hit in the face with a rifle butt by one of the men watching us.

"I am a doctor," said James, and he was immediately manhandled into the clinic.

It was terrifying standing there with these vicious men staring at us with malice. We silently prayed that Sally, James, Miriam, the patients and those who had taken refuge with us would be safe.

"Water," said one of the men, pushing me with such force that I fell headlong onto the sun-baked earth skinning my legs, arms and face. I scrambled to my feet as the men laughed, and gave him a bowl of water. Each one in turn did the same thing, pushing me harder and harder until they all had a drink, laughing hysterically at my predicament, giving me the odd kick as I stood up each time, trying to raise my skirt with their feet. My face was skinned—

mainly my nose and forehead—and my chest and knees. My nose was bleeding heavily.

One of the militia tried to smear my blood all over my face and any exposed flesh with his machete, which was absolutely terrifying. He looked me up and down with lecherous eyes, but, thankfully, he did not sexually assault me.

I told Carl not to do anything, as I knew he would be treated even more violently if he did. The men raised their machetes in the air and swung them with complete abandon. They had modern guns slung over their shoulders.

Time dragged, and we heard dreadful screaming coming from the clinic. It sounded like Miriam. The militiamen watched us, laughing maniacally at our terror.

After four hours, the men came out of the clinic carrying one of our stretchers on which was a patched up, heavily sedated man. Those carrying him were laughing. They loaded him into the truck and drove off, firing their guns into the air.

When we went to the Mission Hall, we found that several families had run away to hide.

Carl, Harry and I dashed over to the clinic where we found that the patients were unhurt, but Sally was dishevelled and ashen with the beginnings of a large bruise forming on her cheek. James had swelling under his right eye where the rifle butt landed. Worst of all, Miriam had been raped by two of the men.

We helped Miriam walk to the house where she had a long bath. She did not utter a word. Sally said, "Miriam is in a catatonic state. I have given her a strong tranquiliser, but there is nothing we can do for the poor girl other than pray for her and show her our love. Poor child, she has been violated in the worst possible way."

Sarah said, "I think one of us should be with her all the time as she might try to do something to herself. I doubt this, but we must make sure she doesn't." She was nearly in tears as she spoke.

"I will stay with her," I said

Sarah and James treated my hands, face and knees, even though they were both shattered. James also started me on a course of antibiotics for fear of my catching any disease through my wounds. Carl got me a large bucket of water, and I washed all the blood off my face, legs and body, and put my clothes in to soak.

I spent the night with Miriam, sitting in an armchair, dropping off periodically but trying desperately to keep my eyes open. Miriam was able to sleep, but she tossed and turned, and at one point, screamed out.

Sadly, the next day, I miscarried our much longed-for baby. I was broken hearted, but fortunately, did not have severe blood loss and felt I was able to continue to care for Miriam, who was gradually beginning to talk and pray.

Sally, however, over-ruled me and said either Harry or Carl could watch Miriam. She insisted I have bed rest, at least for the rest of the day. I was relieved to be alone with my thoughts and prayers and to shed tears for my lost baby.

Harry was the first to bring up the subject of us leaving.

"What will happen to those who need us?" Sally said, mainly to herself.

"What will happen to all of us?" James mused. "Alice has lost her baby, and we are not going to get any more supplies. The militia helped themselves to the majority of our medicines, leaving us short of even the very basics!" Glaring at Carl, he said, "Where is your God now?"

Carl remained calm and composed in his reply. "We vowed to help all those in need when we became Army Officers, and we must do so and not just give up at the first hurdle."

"For fuck's sake, Carl, be realistic. I am sure your God does not want you to sacrifice all our lives. Sorry about the language, but you don't seem to realise that we are all going to be killed if we stay here. Prayers are no protection against machetes and guns."

"What do you think?" Carl asked, looking at Sally and Harry. "Should we leave?"

"Personally, I think we should leave in the short term," was Sally's reply. "The remaining patients are well enough to care for themselves now, and once things have calmed down, we can come back. If we decamp to Juba, we can return as soon as they have the militia under control. She shook her head in despair. "I think that we will do more harm than good staying here, because the militia would take the slaughter of missionaries as a notch in their belts."

"I think we should discuss this with the locals who will be remaining," I added.

James looked stunned that I would even consider this. "Good grief, Alice, they are better off staying here than going back to any of their villages, that is if any of their villages still exist, which I doubt" he exclaimed.

Finally, we decided to go to Juba. We had an old Land Rover, and, taking as little as we could, we left for the twenty-five-mile journey, all feeling scared and praying that we would not encounter any of the militia. Thankfully, we did not.

We arrived safely at our Headquarters in Juba in February 1968. The situation there was virtually civil war, with atrocities being committed throughout Southern Sudan. The Government army seemed completely inadequate and, in fact, some had joined the militia, while others had run away.

We all settled into running a much larger Mission, with a much larger clinic and a resident anaesthetist, much to James's delight, and several volunteer doctors. Carl and I were responsible for the well-being of the bereaved, the orphans and those recovering from life-changing injuries. We also carried out the Sunday services and nightly prayers.

James became more disillusioned by our faith as more and more catastrophic injuries and cruelties occurred.

It was August 1968 and time for James to go back to England to be replaced by another newly qualified doctor from The Royal London Hospital, Whitechapel. We would miss him and his frequent rants about our religious beliefs. His replacement turned out to be a young Irish girl, Maria O'Keefe, from Dublin. Maria had the most beautiful red hair and deep green eyes.

Sally and Harry also returned home in September 1968, I think quite exhausted. We promised to keep in touch, and they both said they would send as much medical equipment, mosquito nets and general supplies as they possibly could get their hands on.

I had several letters from Carol and Ian, and their generosity overwhelmed me. I tried to tell them how much these items meant to the patients, clinic and doctors, but words failed me. I know deep down Carol realised how much they were appreciated.

The next three months went by reasonably peacefully. The hospital had to treat some of the militia but not on a massive scale. The staff became quite relaxed.

In January, Juba was attacked heavily. The hospital and clinics were manic. People were brought in with indescribable injuries, even tiny babies and children. They were all in agony, petrified and some catatonic.

Somewhere in the back of my mind, I could hear James asking how God could let this happen to these tiny little souls.

There were so many traumatized patients that Commissioner Wallace contacted the Headquarters in London to see if they could send psychiatrists and psychologists as a matter of extreme urgency. Obviously this was a big ask, as volunteers risked their lives. The situation was volatile even on the best of days.

We did have guards, courtesy of the local Government, but these seemed a rather motley crew, surly and resentful. Some of them were just as frightened as we were, and several disappeared, whether to join the militia or to hide, we had no idea. None seemed at all shocked by the atrocities; in fact, they seemed to take them as the normal result of conflict.

These attacks were not continuous, but when they did occur, it was mayhem. We were fortunate enough to be able to send the worst casualties to the UK. Miriam accompanied the patients, and it seemed to help her recover. It was an added bonus having such an efficient and knowledgeable nurse to accompany them.

On one of these evacuations, Carol met up with Miriam to get the details on how we were all doing. She asked Miriam to try to get us to go on leave. This just was not possible at this time, but a few weeks later, Maria was going to escort three children to Great Ormond Street, and Carl was going with her to attend a meeting at Headquarters regarding this human crisis. Carol and Ian managed to see Carl though not for long, as he was in meetings at Headquarters and with the Foreign Secretary.

Maria was also going to attend this particular meeting. The Foreign Secretary promised quite a lot of practical aid and said what a wonderful job The Salvation Army was doing.

Carl and Maria arrived back two weeks later with lots of desperately needed supplies. They both seemed well-rested after their break. Carl said that both Carol and Ian looked very well, and he encouraged me to go and stay a couple of days with them if another patient needed to be evacuated.

This happened in August when a little boy needed plastic surgery for terrible burns inflicted by the militia when they had tried to set him on fire. Carol met Miriam and me at Great Ormond Street. It was wonderful to see her, and it was hard to stop cuddling.

"I can't wait to hear all your news!" Carol said excitedly. "You will come and stay with us too, Miriam won't you."

"I would like that," said Miriam as she started up the stairs. "I was actually wondering whether to apply for the post of a Staff Nurse whilst I'm here. I have my qualifications with me, just in case I can get some Agency work until a permanent position turns up."

I added, "I really don't know what we will do without you, but I think this probably is meant to be."

"I'm ready for my bed if you don't mind," said Miriam wearily.

"Me too," I said. "It is going to be wonderful being able to go to sleep knowing nothing is going to happen and we are safe." I fell asleep virtually as soon as my head hit the pillow and slept like a log.

"Wakey, wakey, sleepyhead," sang Carol standing by my bed with a cup of tea.

"What time is it then?"

"Eleven o'clock," said Carol laughing. "You must have been completely exhausted."

I felt really refreshed and ready to get going on my errands for the Mission. I had to go to Headquarters to give a report and organise the delivery of essential supplies for the hospital and staff.

"Miriam has already gone. She wanted to get to the Agencies as early as possible, as she only has a couple of days. I expect it will be form filling, and then she will probably have to come back for interviews."

"Don't rub it in," I said laughing.

I quickly showered, put on my tropical uniform, gulped down a mug of delicious coffee, and set off for Headquarters.

"Good morning, Major Parry," said Brigadier Malony. "How are you?"

"I am very well. Thank you," I answered brightly.

After I gave my report and dealt with the ordering of the supplies, I had a cup of tea with Brigadier Malony.

"How is Carl? We have not seen him for ages. The last time he was here, he left the report and orders for supplies with the office and left. I did not get to see him."

"He is well but very busy like the rest of us at the Mission."

"Give him my good wishes when you get home."

Making my way back to Carol's, I thought it strange when she told me that Carl had stayed at Headquarters whilst he was here last, and that in the two weeks he was here, he only managed to see Carol and Ian once for a meal.

Miriam was already back from the Agencies and had, in fact, got an Agency nursing post at Great Ormond Street to commence the following week.

"What am I going to do without you?" I whined.

"You, my dear Alice, will do fine, as you always do." Miriam was so happy you could not help but feel happy for her too.

When we sat in our pyjamas drinking tea that evening, Carol said, "Well, give me all the gen." I launched into a diatribe of all the happenings at Maroon and Juba. "It must have been terrifying," she said, holding my hand tightly.

"It was, but even more so for the Sudanese who were butchered mercilessly."

The next day Carol and I took the twins to London Zoo, and whilst we were wandering around, Carol asked me if anything was wrong.

"I don't know . . . ." I replied, my voice trailing off. I paused to consider my words. "When Carl was here for the two weeks, he did not stay at Headquarters, nor did he see Brigadier Maloney. He apparently just dropped his report and orders for supplies at the office then departed, and he only visited you and Ian the one time."

"He did see the Foreign Secretary, though, didn't he?" said Carol.

"Yes, but that was for only a few hours."

"I'm sure there is a plausible explanation, Alice dear," Carol said reassuringly.

I had to start packing for my journey back to Juba in the morning. I would be returning alone, because Miriam was staying to work at Great Ormond Street Hospital.

Carol and Ian had arranged a babysitter for the evening, and we all went out for a lovely meal. It was quite a solemn evening, as I was sorry to be leaving, especially without Miriam. When I left in the morning, it was rather a tearful occasion. Carol didn't want me to go and pleaded for me to get a posting back in the UK.

When I arrived at Juba airport, Carl was there and picked me up and hugged me as if I had been away for weeks, not just a couple of days!

While we were driving back to the Mission, I asked how things were, and Carl said, "It has been amazingly quiet, no attacks, and there seems to be a lot more Government troops around."

"Are you shocked that Miriam has stayed in London to work?" I said.

"Not really—she has had a pretty rough time, hasn't she?" replied Carl.

"Brigadier Malony sends his regards and said he was sorry not to see you during your two weeks in the UK," I said, putting it out there to see how Carl would respond. I thought Carl flushed slightly but I may have imagined this. "Where did you stay?" I asked, keeping my voice as casual as possible. "I thought you stayed at Headquarters."

"Actually, Maria's parents very kindly invited me to stay with them in their London flat," Carl said, looking straight ahead, more focused on the road than was necessary.

"How kind of them," I said flatly. We drove in silence until we reached the Mission.

"Here we are, darling, back to the grind," Carl said a bit too lightly, helping me from the car and getting my case. As we walked towards our quarters, Commissioner Wallace came to ask after Miriam.

When I told him about her new nursing post, he said, "Our loss is their gain. I am sure she will be a valued member of the staff at Great Ormond Street."

"Definitely, she is starting work straight away," I said.

"I'll let you get on, Alice. Good to have you back."

I walked towards the clinic to see the patients.

"Don't you want a cup of tea or something?" said Carl.

I shook my head. As I entered, Maria was just coming out.

"Hello, Alice, how time flies—it seems like you were only here this morning," she said with a definite edge to her voice. When I told Carl about this, he said, "I told you to have a break before going to see the patients. You are tired, and I am sure you imagined it. Maria is not like that at all."

I did have a rest and actually dropped off to sleep for a while. I got up and washed and changed into my tropical uniform. I looked out the window and saw Carl and Maria deep in conversation near the clinic, and as I watched, Carl took her hand, looking about furtively. I felt sick. What was happening?

I visited all the patients and held a prayer meeting, but it was a great effort to concentrate. I said goodnight to everyone and went to our quarters. Carl was sitting there reading.

"What is going on, Carl?" I asked.

"What do you mean by that?" he said, trying to sound innocent.

"I saw you and Maria earlier when you thought I was still sleeping. I saw you holding hands."

"What is wrong with that? We're friends."

I took a deep breath to steady myself. "Did you or did you not have more than a friendship whilst you were in England? Tell the truth, Carl. I at least deserve that."

"I am so sorry, Alice, but I just don't love you anymore, not as a wife, but I care for you as a friend."

I was so astounded by Carl's answer that I was speechless. After a few moments of stony silence, I said, "Do you love Maria?"

"Yes." With that, Carl got up and left the room. I was absolutely stunned. What should I do? Obviously, I could not stay in Juba. I went to see Commissioner Wallace and explained, tearfully, the situation.

"Are you quite sure, Alice?" he asked when I was finished.

"Yes, Carl told me to my face—there is no mistake."

PART 5

I told the Commissioner, "I would like to go home as quickly as possible, please. I still have a flat, and I need time to recover from this."

The Commissioner managed to get a call through to Carol, and I explained the whole sorry tale between several sobs.

"I nearly said something to you when you were here, as both Ian and I thought there was something untoward going on when Carl and Maria were both here, but we just could not believe that Carl, a dedicated Christian, would act so abominably. Will you come and stay with us?"

"No, thank you, Carol. I still have my little flat, and I have so much to consider before making any plans. I will be getting a flight home in the next few days and will ring you when I'm back."

I explained my plans to Commissioner Wallace, and he thanked me for all my hard work. "Don't lose your faith, Alice. We will all pray for you."

So in September 1969, I returned home after a traumatic time in Southern Sudan and the devastating blow of being told by my husband that he did not love me. We had only been married for such a short time. I spent the first few days wallowing in misery, and then I suddenly seemed filled with inner strength.

I got in touch with Carol, and we arranged to meet up. "You poor darling," were her first words.

"It's something that I must cope with," I said. "It happens to so many, and I am strong both mentally and physically. I have my own home and many options ahead of me. First of all, though, I am going to have a good rest and pamper myself."

"Good for you, Alice. Ian and I knew you would be strong, but it must be devastating for you. What a rat Carl is!"

"I think I am going to try and forget Carl, hard as it will be. He broke my heart, but he also broke his vows, too, which is a sin."

"You really are a great stoic," said Carol, giving me a quick hug. "I am going to arrange an evening with Miriam when you're up to it which will be great."

"I'll look forward to it. The sooner I get on with my life, the better." I answered. Carol put her hands on her hips, all brisk efficiency. "Right, then, I will try to arrange it for next Saturday, nineteenth September."

This she did, and they both came to my little flat on Primrose Hill, and we had a good time together with lots of laughter.

On Sunday, I went to Central Hall in Oxford Street where no one knew my circumstances. I had to wear my tropical uniform as most of my things had to be posted. The congregation was interested to hear about Juba, and members wanted to know what they could do to help the Mission there. I told them that mosquito nets were vital, as were all medicines and, of course, money for food and water. I gave them the address of the Mission, and I was sure these items would be sent.

I had no intention of going again to Central Hall. I intended to go to Headquarters to see if anyone was wanted in the social side of things, and found that I was in luck.

"We need someone in one of the children's homes as house mother at the end of October for a few weeks," said Brigadier Maloney who obviously knew my circumstances.

"I would love to do that," I replied.

Situated in Battersea, Sunnydays, the children's' home, was mainly for orphans and those taken into care. It had only twenty residents so they could receive the best care possible. I was really looking forward to starting there, but I felt tired although I had had plenty of rest.

I had heard nothing from Carl nor had anyone at the Mission. Obviously, he would have had to leave the Mission and his Commission. Maria would obviously leave the Mission with Carl.

At the end of September, Carol and I went on a trip to Venice for a week. Venice is stunning and the hotel was beautiful. Unfortunately, I had bouts of sickness whilst we were there. Carol looked at me rather strangely and said, "Are you pregnant Alice?"

I realised that this was a distinct possibility, but it had not entered my mind until she asked. "It's possible," I said, doing a quick calculation. "I haven't had a period for quite some time, but I never even thought about it. I thought it was the trauma of Juba and the shock of my split with Carl."

"I think you must get a pregnancy test done as soon as possible," Carol said, hardly able to contain her excitement. "Come on, we will get one before we go to dinner." So off we went to the pharmacy to collect the predictor. We went back to the hotel so I could do the deed. I came out of the bathroom and announced, "I'm pregnant! Can you believe it? I am so happy."

The rest of the week went slowly, as I was longing to go home to get my pregnancy verified and see how far advanced it was. I was at least three months pregnant, I calculated.

On 8 October, I visited my GP, who confirmed my pregnancy and thought I was about fifteen weeks. Dr Jones said he would make an appointment for me to see the obstetrician. He asked how I was coping, and I told him that I was going to do a stint at Sunnydays Children's Home for a few weeks.

I had an appointment for 14 October at University College Hospital where I would be scanned and undergo blood tests. Carol came with me, and when I had my scan, she asked the radiographer if everything looked fine.

"Yes, everything looks fine, and the foetus is approximately seventeen weeks' gestation," he said.

"Seventeen weeks!" I exclaimed. "That means I have only twenty-three weeks to go." After the scan, I saw the obstetrician who confirmed that all was well. My expected date of delivery was 9 March 1970.

"I'll have to find someone who knits," I said, adding, "I am useless at it."

Carol replied, "In any event, it's much cheaper to buy ready-made than to knit nowadays."

That evening I contacted Brigadier Malony to tell him my news and see if it was still all right for me to go to Sunnydays.

"Of course it is, as long as you keep well," was his reply.

"I don't suppose you have any idea where Carl is?" I enquired. "I really should let him know."

Brigadier Maloney spoke to me with compassion. "I am afraid not, Alice. He obviously was not allowed to remain as an Army Officer, so we have no idea of his whereabouts."

Two weeks later, I arrived at Sunnydays and was given a very warm welcome. The Matron introduced me to the children as Major Parry. "I would like to be called Major Alice or just Alice," I told her.

"Well, I think we should call you Major Alice. We have allocated you to Blue Group, four little ones from the same family who have been taken into care because of physical abuse and malnutrition. This is Sam, who is six. Amy and Emily, the twins, are aged four. And baby Lucy is nine months."

I looked at these four beautiful children and wondered how anyone could hurt them. Again, James's words came to mind.

"Well, treasures," I said, "come and show me where we live, and tell me the things that I am supposed to do."

Sam was the first to speak. "You have to give us our tea, then baths and a bedtime story."

"Right, Sam. What time is tea?"

Sam said, "When you say, I suppose. Lucy has to have a bottle of milk before she goes to bed."

The children took me to our apartment, which was bright and clean and really quite large. There was a living room with two settees, a television, a bookshelf and boxes of toys, a kitchen and three bedrooms—one for the twins and baby, one for Sam and one for me.

I checked the provisions in the kitchen and was pleased there were plenty. "As it is my first day with you, you can choose what you would like for your tea."

Sam said, "Fish fingers and chips."

Amy and Emily didn't say anything, so I put my arms around them and told them to find something they wanted from the fridge and cupboards.

Sam piped up, "They won't tell you. Give them McDonalds—they always eat that." I looked in the freezer and found some good quality beef burgers and some bread buns that would defrost quickly. I decided to make Lucy boiled eggs and soldiers.

In the meantime, we all had juice and chocolate biscuits that I had brought with me. We sat together on one settee with the plate of biscuits on the coffee table in front of us. "Do you know where I worked before I came here?" I asked them.

"Not really," said Sam.

"I worked in Africa," I said, hoping to pique their interest.

"Where's that?" said Sam.

I got up with Lucy sitting on my hip and went to the bookshelf to see if there was a book to help me explain this to them.

Fortunately, there was a Johnny Morris book about African animals, which also contained a map suitable for small children. I showed them the pictures of the animals found throughout Africa and pictures of deserts, as well as some pictures of Sudanese children. This seemed to keep them interested at least for a short while. It was obvious that Lucy needed her nappy changed, so I suggested that the older children have their baths, and then I would make their meal.

Amy and Emily had not made a sound, and Lucy was very docile for an infant of nine months. I wondered what these lovely children had been through. After their baths, when they were all snug in their jimjams watching the television, I set to making their meal. When it was ready, I called through from the kitchen for them to sit up. I put Lucy in her high chair. She smelt lovely with Johnson's Baby Talc liberally applied by her sisters. They even smiled as they sat down but still did not speak. Sam, however, did.

"Cor, I've got four fish fingers!" he exclaimed, and tucked in as if he hadn't eaten a proper meal in ages. They ate all what was in front of them and had some fresh fruit afterwards.

I made Lucy a bottle of milk, and we all sat down for thirty minutes of children's television. When Lucy fell asleep in my arms, I put her in her cot. Returning to the children, I said, "Would you like me to read you a story?"

"If you want," said Sam, still the spokesman for the family.

I read a couple of chapters from *Bright Eyes* and then went with them to their bedrooms. Sam jumped into his bed and snuggled in. Amy and Emily got into their beds. I said a little prayer for them and kissed them goodnight. I went back to Sam's room and said a little prayer for him too. I bent to kiss him, but he turned away and said, "Yuck."

Later that evening, the Matron came to see if all had gone well. "Yes, they are as good as gold," I reported. "The twins have not said a word though."

"I'm afraid they are probably too frightened to speak," replied Matron. "They were beaten by their father if they said much."

I decided now was as good a time as any to talk to Matron about my circumstances. "I meant to tell you earlier but did not get the chance. I am pregnant, due in March next year."

I saw the surprise on Matron's face.

I hastened to add, "I was married, but whilst working in Africa, my husband told me he no longer loved me and loved someone else."

"Oh, I see," she said, letting out the breath she had been holding. "You poor dear. Make sure you let me know if things get too much for you." Her smile was genuine.

After she left, I went to bed and slept well, and the children were quiet all through the night

The following morning, a school day for Sam and nursery school for the twins, Sam came through to the kitchen.

"Good morning, Sam," I greeted him. "Are the girls awake?"

"Think so, and Lucy's gurgling away."

I went through to the girls' bedroom and, sure enough, they were all awake. "Come on, my treasures, time to rise and shine," I said as I got Lucy up from her cot.

The twins didn't move. "I can see someone is going to have to be tickled," I said jovially. Emily started to cry and, as I went to her, she cowered in fear. I picked her up and felt immediately that she was soaking wet, as was the bed. "Don't cry, darling, it really doesn't matter. Most little children wet the bed. So do some grownups."

To my surprise, she clung to me tightly. Sam said, "They got beat by Dad and locked in a cupboard if they wet the bed."

"Well, I can promise you that nothing like that will happen to you again."

Emily calmed down, and we had breakfast and then got ready for school and nursery. "Has everybody cleaned their teeth?" I asked.

"Yes" the children answered in unison.

The school was very close to Sunnydays, and the nursery was an integral part of the main school.

Once I had Lucy safely buckled into her pram, we set off for the school. Amy and Emily actually asked if I would be picking them up after school. "Of course I will, right on time. I thought maybe we could have a picnic in the park as long as the weather keeps fine."

"Yes, please," Sam answered for them all.

When I got back to our home, the Matron came to see me. "What day do you have to go for your ante-natal clinic so I can arrange cover?"

"November twentieth at ten, so I can take the children to school, and collect them in the afternoon as normal. Have you any idea when they will be fostered?"

"I think before Christmas. They are fortunately the type of family that is easy to place."

"I am so pleased to hear that, Matron. They are beautiful children, and hopefully I can care for them until then. They won't be split up, will they?"

"No. It is our ruling that families must be kept together."

I spoke to Carol during the morning and gave her an update. "You must bring them to tea with the twins on Saturday, eighth November," she said. "I am sure they will love to come and play in the garden, and I'm looking forward to seeing you all too."

As promised, we had a picnic in the park that afternoon, and the children played on the swings, slides and roundabout. We stayed for a couple of hours, and then Lucy began to get grumpy, so we made our way back home.

On Wednesday, 5 November, whilst the children were at school and I was playing with Lucy, Matron arrived. "We have a placement for the children. They are coming to collect them on Saturday," she said happily.

"So soon—I'm just gaining their trust," I said, disappointed.

"They are going to a lovely couple who will love them very much."

"Do I tell them?"

"Definitely not. We introduce them to the foster parents, and they take them the same day—it is less traumatic for the children," Matron said.

"Will they see their parents at all?" I enquired.

"I would doubt that," was Matron's answer. "They are both in prison."

Lucy was trying to get our attention. "Do you want to play, Lucy?" I asked as she pulled herself up and put a toy brick in my lap. "Come on then," I said, and as soon as I put the bricks one on top of the other, a chubby little hand knocked them over with a delightful giggle and a dribbly smile, as she was cutting more teeth.

Matron got up and made her way to the door. She stopped before opening it and said, "Lucy seems to be coping well since she arrived here."

"Yes, she sleeps and feeds well, but Amy and Emily hardly speak, and are terrified if they do anything they think is wrong, such as spilling their juice. Sam told me their father beat them and locked them in a cupboard as punishment. I think Sam was treated cruelly too, but he puts it to the back of his mind. He is protective of all the girls, but I worry that he is hiding his own bad treatment."

"Well, soon they will be part of a lovely family with older siblings, two of which are junior doctors."

The next two days went by uneventfully. On Saturday, I bathed the children and put them in their best clothes. When I finished changing Lucy's nappy, Matron arrived with a lovely looking couple, probably in their late forties, with their teenage daughter.

"Come and meet your new family, children," said Matron, and they obeyed immediately and were introduced one by one. Lucy was immediately taken from my arms and put into the arms of her new mummy. The twins were cuddled and kissed, and Sam screwed up his face when receiving his cuddle and kiss, but I am sure he really enjoyed it.

They all said goodbye, apart from Lucy, of course.

As I watched them leave, with a lump in my throat, I hoped that they would be loved and cared for the rest of their lives. Following their departure, I called Carol. I had already told her that we would not be coming for tea, but Carol said, "Well, you can still come, can't you, and we can have a good gossip."

"Will it be okay for me to come around five?" I asked.

"Absolutely—see you later."

After the family had left with Sam, Amy, Emily and Lucy, Matron came to see me. "What are your plans now, Alice? At the moment, we have no other family without a housemother."

"I thought I would have a good rest, go back to my own flat and try to find out where Carl is. He needs to know about the baby. I will have to start making preparations too for the delivery."

Matron gave me a warm smile. "You have been marvellous with the children, Alice. I don't really think you know how much you helped them. We will all miss you and wish you well with the birth of your own child and success in finding out where the father is."

"Thank you, Matron," I said. "Is it all right if I go now? I would rather not hang around."

"Yes, of course. Thank you very much for all you've done. Goodbye, Alice." With that, Matron left the apartment, and I gathered the few things I had brought with me and set off to Primrose Hill.

PART 6

Once I let myself into the flat and opened the windows to let fresh air in, I felt so forlorn that I started to cry and could not stop. I felt utterly alone in the world. Why had Carl left me? As hard as I tried, I could think of no logical reason other than the fact that he obviously never loved me in the first place. I loved him and he knew this. Why was all this terrible suffering going on in the world—the terrible cruelty dealt from man to man, the neglect and killing of so many children throughout the world, including here in the UK?

My crying gradually subsided, but I was physically exhausted. I was about to lie down when my doorbell rang. It was Carol come to pick me up for a change. "What on earth is the matter, Alice?" she exclaimed after taking one look at me.

"Oh, Carol, I feel so sad. There are so many dreadful things happening in this world. I miss Carl desperately. What am I going to do?"

"First of all, you are going to pull yourself together and remember that you have a darling new baby on the way. Stop thinking of others more than yourself, especially that rat Carl. Go and wash your face. We are going to my house, and then, my girl, we are going to the theatre." Carol always had a domineering way, but she meant well and loved me dearly. "You must try to forget what Carl has done. It is his loss. He obviously was not a very good Christian, was he? We will find him. Don't you worry."

Again, James's words and arguments came to mind: "Why does your God let these terrible things happen?"

The evening went very well. We had a lovely meal, and then we went to see *Mousetrap*. Carol was amazed that I had never seen it, because it had been running so long. I went straight home following the theatre. I had a bath, and then went to bed and again started crying, but I finally fell asleep, emotionally drained from so many things that had occurred that day.

The following morning I awoke early to the noise of the milkman, which was lucky because I had no milk. I caught him as he was delivering next door. "Have you a spare pint of milk?" I asked hopefully. "I also need bread, butter and eggs."

"Anything for you, Major. Are you back for good now?"

I shrugged my shoulders, not sure how to answer.

"Glad to see you back again, anyhow, love."

I made tea, toast and scrambled eggs and began to think rationally. Grampy Martin had left me quite well off financially. I would have to start looking for a bigger house, although I doubted I would be able to afford to stay in the Primrose Hill area, but you never know. The phone rang, and it was Brigadier Maloney. "Hello Alice," he said when I answered the call. "We have found out the whereabouts of Carl, and as per usual, we have written to him asking him to contact you. You realise I cannot send Carl's details directly to you."

"Of course, Brigadier. Thank you for your help. I will just have to hope he will be gentleman enough to contact me." I knew this would happen.

"I wish you luck," Brigadier said. "I hope all is going well with your pregnancy, and I will pray for you and your baby." After that, he said goodbye.

It was now Sunday, 9 November, and I had no inclination to go to an Army service and, shamefully, felt no guilt. I checked around the flat. Everything was in good condition, but I would get an estate agent to give me a valuation on it. Then I would be able to start looking around for a home for me and my baby. I had no doubt that Carol would accompany me on this quest.

I was due to go to the prenatal clinic on 20 November, and, until then, I would look for a nice house for the baby and me.

Brigadier Maloney called me on 11 November to see if I would cover for a Corps in Kent, but I declined. I did not even have to think about it. I told him that I would be taking a furlough as I had not taken one since first going to the East End. He seemed rather surprised at my declination and said if I changed my mind to get in touch with him, sooner rather than later. As an afterthought, he said, "Bye the bye, have you heard from Carl yet?" I said that I hadn't and we said goodbye and rang off.

The following day the estate agent called to say that a Victorian terrace house had just come onto the market. Apparently, it needed complete updating but was structurally sound and, best of all, in my price range and in Primrose Hill. I arranged to see it the next day at noon and asked Carol to go with me. Obviously, she was delighted to do so, and we met up outside the large terraced Victorian house at the same time.

The agent arrived shortly after. When we entered the house, I was stunned by all the original features: the lovely tiled floor in the porch and hallway, the high ceilings and beautiful original cornicing and plaster work. The rooms were large and airy. The kitchen was large, but would need complete renovation. There were fireplaces in all the rooms, but there was no central heating, and the bathroom needed updating, but that could wait for a while. I thought that my project, whilst waiting to deliver, would be to decorate as much as I was able and then see what I could afford later.

"Carol, this is it," I said, as we stood near one of the bedroom windows taking in the view. "This is my new home. I love it."

"There's an awful lot to do," she said. "You must get the electrics checked and the roof and attic, too."

"I will have a full survey, and if it is favourable, I would like to buy it," I said to both the estate agent and Carol. "My offer is ten thousand pounds less than the asking price because the house needs a lot of work. The kitchen must be updated, and central heating definitely must be installed as a matter of expediency."

Carol and I went back to my flat. "How on earth are you going to furnish such a big house?" she asked.

"Room by room, as—and when—I can afford it," I said excitedly. "The agent said he would get in touch with the owners and let me know whether they accept my offer."

I could hardly wait for the answer from the agent. In fact, I did not have to wait long, as the answer came the following day—it was a yes.

I phoned Carol immediately, and she seemed as excited as I. I contacted my solicitor to tell him to go ahead with the conveyancing. My little flat sold immediately and for more than I was asking, as there were several people interested in buying it. Now all I had to do was be patient and wait for it all to go through.

I attended the prenatal clinic on Thursday, and all was well. The baby was growing nicely, and I was fit and healthy.

On Sunday, 23 November, I decided to go and see how my first little Corps in the East End was doing, quite a journey but something I wanted to do. I went by tube and arrived well in time for the 11.00 o'clock morning service.

When I entered the hall, I was so pleased to see quite a substantial number of bandsmen, songsters and congregation. I also saw Maggie, to my delight. She didn't see me immediately, but when she did, she came running over and wrapped her skinny arms around me.

"Major Parry! I didn't think I would ever see you again. Where's your husband? Are you up the duff?" Maggie hardly took a breath.

"Give me a chance, Maggie!" I said, and we shared a laugh. "I am so pleased to see you, too. Yes, I am up the duff, as you call it, and I do not know where my husband is. There, that's all your questions answered. Now my turn. How old are you now? How is your Mum and the baby?"

"I am nearly eleven, and me Mum and baby are well. The baby is a toddler now and quite fat. Me dad did not come back, luckily, and we have moved to a new house on a new estate. How do you mean you don't know where your husband is?"

"He didn't want to live with me anymore, Maggie. I don't know why."

"He must be doolally, stupid man," was Maggie's retort.

"We had better sit down now, Maggie, the meeting is just starting."

The young officers reminded me of Carl and me when we first started out. It was a lovely service, and when it was over, I had a chat with Captain and Mrs. Jones. I told them of my first days in the little corps. Of course, it was bigger now, partly due to my efforts, I hoped.

"Does Kitty still attend here?" I asked Captain Jones.

"I am sorry to say that she passed away quite recently. Unfortunately, she had carcinoma of the colon, and it was not discovered in time," he replied.

"I am sorry to hear this. She was a great help to me." I told him of all the work she did making the Sunbeam uniforms fit all the children after we obtained them from bigger Corps. "Maggie became a Sunbeam and literally helped herself to food for those in need, although she did not realise that was actually stealing. I am sure the local tradesmen turned a blind eye to her antics."

Mrs. Jones said, "Maggie takes the Sunbeams now. She is a great asset to the Corps."

"It was lovely meeting you both and to see how the Corps is gaining in numbers, but I must be off." I went to Maggie to say goodbye. "I am so glad to hear that you are now taking the Sunbeams. I will be moving soon, but if you give me your address, I will send you my new address so we can keep in touch."

"Okay, I'll get some paper," said Maggie. She shot off and was back before I knew it. "There you are, Major Parry. Don't forget, will you."

"Of course I won't, and please call me Alice."

"Right-o! See you soon then."

When I got home, I had some lunch and started to pack up some of my things, which took considerable time because it brought back so many memories, both happy and sad.

I had an early night and got up ready to put my back into the packing. The postman brought a letter from Carl saying that Brigadier Malony had asked him to get in touch with me. He said I could ring him at his workplace during his lunch hour, about 1.00 p.m., as he was now teaching in a secondary school in Kent. He gave me the number but not the name of the school or his home address. I decided to take the bull by the horns and phone him today. I packed until 1.00 p.m., but the time dragged. At last, it was time to call him. I dialled the number with my heart pounding in my chest.

A strange voice answered. "Staff room."

"Can I speak to Mr. Parry, please?"

"Hold on, I'll get him. Can I say who is calling?"

"Yes, it's Alice." It seemed quite a while before Carl came on the phone. "Hi, Alice, I hope all is well with you. Brigadier Malony said you had something to discuss with me."

"I won't waste your time, Carl, but the important matter I wish to discuss with you is that I am pregnant, due in March. I am buying a new house in Primrose Hill and will be moving soon."

After what seemed a long time, Carl finally spoke. "This does not alter the situation, but I will support you financially as best I can. Can you phone me when you move?"

"If that is what you want. By the way, all seems to be well with the baby." With that, I put the phone down. I could not believe how cold Carl had been. He hadn't even asked about his own child.

I phoned Carol and told her my news. "Don't get in touch with him again. He obviously seems disinterested—I just can't believe it, callous sod!" Carol could not hide her anger. "Do you want me to come over?"

"No, thanks, Carol. I actually don't feel the least bit upset—this is exactly what I expected."

The next two days went by uneventfully, and the estate agent phoned to say that everything had gone through on both properties, and would I pop in to my solicitors to sign all the necessary documents. I arranged to go the following morning and felt very excited about the move to my new home.

The following morning everything was signed and sealed; all I had to do was arrange a removal company. The terrace house was already empty, and I was lucky to get a removal company that could move my small amount of belongings the next day! So, on 25 November, I arrived in my new home. I could not wait to get started on transforming the rather neglected house. Carol, of course, arrived armed with cleaning products and large tins of magnolia paint and paintbrushes. "I thought we could use this magnolia paint just to brighten up the living room and hall until you can do it all properly."

"I can always count on you, Carol!" I said with a laugh. She was the picture of brisk efficiency. Looking around with hands on hips, I said, "I must get a quote for the kitchen as soon as possible, as that is the worst room, and it needs to be done professionally."

Ian arrived dressed in overalls and armed with a ladder. He was "allowed" to paint the ceiling roses and cornices after he had brushed off the dust and cobwebs. It seemed that within no time at all, the living room had a nice clean ceiling and cornices, and magnolia walls. I had three armchairs and a settee in duck-egg blue, a coffee table, and a small glass cabinet that belonged to Nanny and Grampy Martin. Once those were arranged, the room looked welcoming and cosy. The floor was parquet flooring, which I had professionally polished, so no carpet would be needed, but a nice Persian rug would look lovely.

We went out to dinner after the hard work Carol and Ian had done. Their twins, Christopher and Isobel, were looked after by Carol's mum. We enjoyed a relaxed meal and light-hearted conversation, and it was quite late when we went to our respective homes.

The following day, I wrote to Maggie and told her my new address. I then went to some do-it-yourself outlets to look at the kitchens. I found the one I wanted and arranged for it to be delivered and fitted, but that could not be done until after Christmas. Fortunately, the central heating was put in at the beginning of December.

My December prenatal appointment found me fit and well. I had made an effort to get the baby's room ready, although I had plenty of time, and, with the newly installed central heating, I was warm and snug.

Naturally, Carol had invited me for Christmas, so I was off shopping for presents for Christopher, Isobel, Carol and Ian. I would also get a gift for Maggie.

When I returned home and was enjoying a cup tea, Brigadier Maloney rang. "Hello, Alice. How are you keeping?"

"I'm remarkably well and getting the house in order," I answered cheerily.

"Excellent news, Alice," he said. After a slight pause, he added, "Have you heard from Carl yet?"

"Yes, he sent me his telephone number for the school he is working at so I managed to tell him about the baby. I'm afraid there was not a positive response, and I haven't heard from him since."

"Have you decided what you are going to do after the baby is born? Will you want to be placed in another Corps? You cannot remain a commissioned officer unless you take up a posting."

"I'm afraid I really do not know if that is what I want," I answered.

As soon as I spoke those words, I realised that I felt no enthusiasm or calling to continue in this field. Perhaps it was my hormones. I wasn't sure, but the enthusiasm for this work was gone.

"I am sorry to hear that, Alice," said Brigadier Maloney. "Think long and hard before you make your final decision."

I was rather surprised by the tone of his voice.

Christmas came and went, and the kitchen was installed. I had had an uneventful prenatal visit with only eight weeks to go before the baby was born.

I still had not heard a word from Carl, nor had I heard anything further from the Brigadier. I had seen Maggie who was delighted with her gift, a nice leather shoulder bag. Even she quizzed me about my future. "You can't give it up, Alice. You were so good at what you did."

I had no inclination to go to the Army, and I eventually wrote to the Brigadier to let him know I no longer wanted to be involved. Carol was pleased with my decision and said, "Once that baby is born, you won't have a minute to spare."

My Precious Sunbeam

By the time my February hospital appointment came, I was waddling. I seemed to have grown huge overnight, but all was well medically. I had so many baby-grows in all sizes that I could have dressed a nursery.

Dear Maggie knitted a darling little matinee jacket with an intricate pattern. "What beautiful knitting, Maggie!" I exclaimed when I opened the parcel. "Who taught you?"

"My Nan. I am teaching the Sunbeams to knit too. Nan is going to help too." I could not help noticing that her grammar, pronunciation and vocabulary had improved as well, but I made no comment.

Carol had me out and about, walking as much as possible, which was very good exercise for me. We laughed a lot, and I felt happy. I thought myself very lucky to have such a lovely home, wonderful friends and, of course, my not so scruffy anymore little Maggie.

During the night of 10 March, I went into labour. I called the ambulance and picked up my bag, packed and ready, and went to University College Hospital where I delivered a 7-pound 8-ounce baby girl at 11.00 a.m., the most beautiful baby I had ever seen. I called Carol, who couldn't believe it and set off immediately to see the new arrival.

"Have you 'phoned Carl yet?" she asked when she arrived at the hospital and had settled into a chair near my bed.

"No, but I am ringing him at one during his lunch break." Carol went and got the telephone trolley, and I rang Carl's school.

"Staff room," answered Carl himself.

"It's Alice—you have a beautiful baby girl."

"Oh. Is she all right?"

"Perfect," I answered proudly.

"I'll try to get over to see her," Carl said in a bland voice. "How long will you be in hospital? What hospital is it?"

I told him that I would be going home the next day. I told him my new address and the hospital address and rang off.

"Pretty interested, eh," said Carol sarcastically. "What a toss pot, why you ever married him I don't know."

"I loved him, Carol."

"He went off and left you before you went to Hungary," Carol reminded me, as if I needed reminding. As it happened, I stayed in hospital for four days.

Maggie came bounding in the day I was going home. "I just got your card. Isn't she lovely! Can I hold her?" she babbled with excitement.

I was a bit nervous of her holding the baby. "I was wondering if you would like to come home with me, and then I will get a taxi to take you home. Would you like that?"

"Would I!" came the delighted reply.

Carol, who was also there, raised her eyebrows and held back a laugh. She knew that I loved Maggie like a daughter.

The four of us arrived home around noon. Maggie unpacked my bags and made us a cup of tea. As we sat around the kitchen table with the baby in her pram, the doorbell rang. Maggie ran to open it. We heard her say, "Oh! It's you, is it? Wait a minute."

She returned to the kitchen and said in a loud whisper, "It's Carl. Shall I let him in?"

"Of course, Maggie," I said, repressing a smile at how protective of me she was.

A rather sheepish Carl entered the kitchen.

"Hello, Carl," Carol said. "You made it then."

Carl gave her a curt nod and looked in my direction. "Hello, Alice. Are you well?"

"Fine, thanks. Do you want a cup of tea or a juice?" I tried to be as normal as possible whilst my heart was in turmoil.

"Nothing, thanks. I'm on my lunch break so haven't much time."

"Your daughter's in the pram if you are interested," said Carol with unmistakable sarcasm.

"Of course I am interested," Carl snapped back and went over to the pram. His face did not move a muscle; there was no reaction at all as he looked down on the sleeping child. "What's her name?" he asked, glancing up at me.

"I don't know yet. I have not decided," I said honestly.

"Do you need anything?" Carl said quietly.

"Yes, I need maintenance. We can either do this through the solicitor or just between ourselves. It is the least you can do."

I couldn't believe I was being so forthright. I think I was fuming that he had shown no emotion when looking at his daughter for the first time. "I think, in fact, it would be more binding if we arranged this through the solicitor. I have his card here and will get in touch with him and ask him to contact you direct," I said.

"How on earth did you manage to buy this beautiful house?"

"You can keep your filthy mitts off the house," Carol snapped. "Alice inherited it, and it has absolutely nothing to do with you."

"I get the message, Carol," he said in a droll tone. He looked at me and said, "I must be going," and made his way to the door. "Tell the solicitor he can only reach me on the school number."

"You were rather nasty, Carol," I said after he left.

"Well, I just told him the truth in case he gets any bright ideas of cashing in on your inheritance. What a cold fish. I really can't believe he is not interested in the baby or you." Carol huffed out an angry breath.

Maggie put her arms around me. "Never mind him, Alice. You've got all of us—we love you." This kind gesture made me weep.

I gradually got into the swing of things, although I never seemed to have time for the routine day-to-day cleaning, as it seemed an endless round of changing nappies, bathing and feeding. Unfortunately, she was not a good sleeper at night, and I felt worn out, but that was a small price to pay for such a God-given treasure. Gradually things improved, and with the unending help of Carol and Maggie, things became much easier.

I decided to call her Anna, and in July, I arranged with Captain and Mrs. Jones at my old corps for her to be dedicated, the Salvation Army equivalent to being christened. This was to take place on 10 July 1970, when Anna would be four months old.

I telephoned Carl to tell him of Anna's dedication. Carol, Ian, Christopher, Isobel and Maggie would be attending. I had also invited Brigadier Malony, and he accepted the invitation readily. I told Carol I had invited Carl, and she couldn't help herself saying, "Why are you inviting that creep after all he has done to you?" I explained that he was Anna's father, and if I didn't ask him, I would be as bad as he was.

Isobel and Maggie wanted to prepare a snack for after the service, as it was a fairly long journey from the East End to Primrose Hill. Carol said, "Don't worry. I will be supervising, and it will be fine." So I agreed. There was no doubting that they all loved Anna very much.

The day of the service arrived. Anna was dressed in the most beautiful dress, courtesy of Carol and Ian. Carl turned up and stood next to me during the service but made no effort to hold Anna and made his excuses to leave as soon as the service was over. "I am afraid I find Carl's actions hard to understand," said Brigadier Malony. "It is so foreign to me to see a father completely disinterested in his own child."

After our lunch, which Carol supervised excellently, we went back to Primrose Hill. Anna went for a sleep, and the rest of us sat around the living room chatting and drinking cups of tea made by Maggie and Isobel.

During a lag in the conversation, Brigadier Malony said to me, "What are you going to do now you have no income?"

"I really have no idea, Brigadier. You're right, I am going to have to earn a living somehow or other."

"I can't persuade you to take on another corps?" the Brigadier said.

"No. I am sorry to say that my faith has been severely dented," I said. "I wouldn't feel right being an officer. I hope things change, as I did love my work."

At 5.00 p.m. or thereabouts, everyone started getting ready to go home. Carol and Ian offered to take Maggie home. Just before Maggie left, she turned and said to me, "I get my Eleven-plus results this week."

"Oh, Maggie, I am sure you will pass. Do you know which Grammar School you will be going to?"

"Hampstead, so I can be nearer to you when I have time to come. I think there will be a lot of homework, and I still want to be involved in my Sunbeam group."

I felt sure she would pass. She was a very bright child and far more mature than her years.

Anna was rather fractious that afternoon. I think she was passed around too much and did not like being swamped by so many people. I bathed her and fed her, and she had that lovely baby smell of Johnson's talc as I settled her down in her cot. She cried a little but soon fell asleep. I, too, must have nodded off, because the next thing I knew the phone was ringing and it was 8.30 p.m.

PART 7

"Hello."

"Is that you Alice?" I was surprised to hear an unfamiliar male voice at the other end of the phone.

"Yes it is. I don't recognise the voice. I'm sorry."

"It's James. I was with you and Carl in the Sudan."

"How lovely to hear from you. How did you find me?"

"I have ways and means," James said in a mock sinister voice. "Is it all right if I come around? I know it's a bit late, but I'm dying to see you both." I wondered if he meant Anna or Carl in the word both.

"Yes, that's fine, but don't be too late. I go to bed rather early."

"No prob. I am actually outside now." I rushed to open the front door and there he stood, handsome, healthy and far more mature looking than I remembered.

"Come in, James. Sit down, and I'll make you a cup of tea."

"Give me a kiss first, Alice." I did, and surprised myself at how excited I felt kissing him. I hadn't thought about him in quite some time, and now there he was, and it seemed as if he was right where he belonged.

We both sat down, tea forgotten.

"How did you find me?" I asked.

"Well, I have been a little naughty actually. I am doing my surgical rotation and was given a particular case to lecture on, and whilst looking up the patient on the microfiche, your name popped up next to the patient concerned. Not allowed, really, but I am sure you won't blab!"

"Of course I won't, James. I'm really happy to see you."

"Where's that pious sod Carl, then?"

"I see your language has not improved. He left me when we were in the Sudan. All I know is the telephone number of the school in Kent where he works. Obviously you know I have a beautiful baby girl called Anna who is four months now. Anna was dedicated today. Carl actually turned up for Anna's dedication but showed no interest whatsoever in her—or me for that matter. He went off with your replacement in Juba. He has never kept in touch, and we had to trace him through the Salvation Army, although, of course, he plays no active role in the Army. He is as cold as ice when he looks at the baby, quite unnatural when he was so good with the children in the East End and the Sudan."

"That is a sign of absolute guilt. I knew he was a hypocrite. Anyway, can I see Anna? I promise I won't waken her."

"Of course you can, James. Let's go up to the nursery."

James's face was tender and in awe of my beautiful baby whilst looking at the little bundle of joy sleeping peacefully in her cot—quite a difference from the expression on Carl's face when he looked at her.

I smiled. "Sadly, this is a false picture, as she plays up a bit during the night."

"Truly she is a beautiful baby, Alice, just like her mum," James said whilst looking directly into my eyes. I felt my cheeks flush but made no comment.

We went downstairs, and I offered him tea or coffee. He declined both and said he would be on his way so I could get to bed but told me he would be visiting again. When I opened the front door, he leant forward and kissed me, and as I responded involuntarily, he put his arms around me and gave me a long, lingering kiss—bliss after having no man in my life for so long and the dreadful feeling of rejection that Carl had visited on me.

"God, I've wanted to do that since the moment I first set eyes on you, Alice," James said huskily. At that moment, there came a cry from upstairs. "Saved by the baby," laughed James. "I will see you soon, but I'll ring first. Still being a junior doctor, I don't get much time off, but I'll see you as soon as I can."

"I hope so too, James. Goodnight."

The following morning, 11 July 1970, after feeding, bathing and dressing Anna, I phoned Carol to tell her of the previous night's events, leaving a little bit out. "Wow, that's a turn-up for the books," Carol said excitedly. "Now make the most of it. We are nearly always available to babysit."

"I am still married to Carl," I said, and, after a slight pause, I added, "I must not forget that."

"Like he has remembered he is married to you, you mean. Has he been to see Anna? No. Has he contacted you at all about helping you with the financial side of bringing up his child? No. It's about time you realised he does not want anything to do with either of you." Carol spoke firmly and unintentionally hurtfully.

"I really don't know what I am going to do. I don't want to continue being an officer, but I can't stop loving the Army. Perhaps there is a niche for me somewhere once Anna is older. I am thinking of doing a nursing course for use in the future. Anyway, I must go. Anna is due at the clinic for her jab—I'm dreading it, poor little mite. Bye, my love, see you soon."

I caught of glimpse of myself in the mirror, and when I took a good look, I realised that even though I was attractive, I could make much more of my appearance. I decided that I would start today. I would first get my blonde hair styled properly and start using conditioner and moisturiser. I went to the clinic, and Anna was weighed and given her jab—she didn't even flinch! After this, I went into the rather plush looking hairdressers in Primrose Hill Road, and they managed to fit me in. Anna was the centre of attention gurgling and smiling—quite an actress! The stylist asked how I would like my hair styled, and I told him that I would leave it to him, as I had no idea what was current. He suggested that I have highlights even though my hair was quite blonde. I said I would be guided by him. At the end of quite a long process, I could not believe the difference—I looked lovely. The stylist, Ben, said, "You look fabulous, Alice. The colour of your hair goes with your peaches-and-cream complexion."

I was quite embarrassed. Anna decided she had had enough of people flattering her mother and started to whine. "I must get her home," I said to Ben, gathering my bag. "She is tired now and wants her feed." Ben handed me the bill, and I was utterly shocked. It was so expensive. I would have to take stock of myself and not be so vain! However, I was delighted with the way I looked, and why shouldn't I have something for myself? I knew Carol would be delighted.

I got home and fed, watered and changed Anna. When I put her down for her nap, I looked through directory enquires to see if any nursing courses were advertised. I had no luck with this and so contacted the Royal College of Nursing, and they told me of an Open University course. I immediately contacted this organisation and registered. This would be absolutely ideal, as I would be working from home and would need babysitters only when I had to attend lectures.

Everything was looking up. It was a new week, a new me and a definite new path to follow.

I saw Carol the following day. "I can't believe my eyes," she said. "You look utterly stunning."

"I have been very extravagant though. I also enrolled in a nursing course with the Open University."

"Oh, Alice, I'm so proud of you. You are an inspiration to us all." Carol wiped a tear from her eye.

On Friday, my first papers arrived from the Open University, and I couldn't wait for Anna to have her nap so I could get started. Once I did, I was absolutely absorbed in it. When Anna got up and had her lunch and was changed, I put her in the pram and walked to the library to get some reference books. *Take it easy*, I told myself. *There is a long way to go, and you don't want to blow yourself out before you get started.*

When I arrived home, Maggie was waiting outside for me. "I passed my Eleven plus!" she shouted before I actually reached her.

"Oh, Maggie, well done," I said, hugging her tightly. "I knew you would. Are you coming in?"

"No, I've got to get home to tell Mum when she gets in from work—and look at you with your new hairdo. You look like a movie star!"

"Thanks, Maggie. I thought it was time for a change. I love it! But do come in, and I will get you a taxi. It is a long way to your home, and this will be my celebratory gift to you. I am so proud of you." After seeing her off, I telephoned Carol to tell her.

"I must send her a little gift as a congratulation," Carol said immediately. "I have a brand new leather satchel in the loft which I am sure she would like."

"I'm sure she would, too," I replied. What a change from a scruffy little Sunbeam to a Grammar School girl. Her mother must be so proud. I wrote her a letter to congratulate her on her clever daughter, and she replied thanking us all for the help we gave Maggie along the way. That evening James phoned to ask if he could come around and bring a take-away. I said that would be great and to come about 8.00 p.m. when, hopefully, Anna would be in the land of Nod.

James arrived just before 8.00 p.m. Anna was not in the land of Nod—far from it. She was fractious and refused to be put down. James said, "Let me have her, and you can put the food in the oven to keep warm."

"I wonder if she will take a little milk," I said.

"If you make her a bottle then, I will try and give it to her," said James.

I made Anna a few ounces of milk, and James managed successfully to give it to her. I put the food on a low heat, and as she was taking her milk, Anna's eyelids started to droop, and she soon fell asleep. We both crept upstairs with her and laid her in her cot.

We ate our meal, and as I put the plates in the dishwasher, James put his arms around me and kissed my neck. I turned around to him and we kissed passionately and urgently. James caressed my breasts, and our kissing became more and more heated. We lay down on the settee. James removed my clothes and looked longingly at me. "Oh, Alice, you are so beautiful. I have thought this since the first time we met in the Sudan." He sat beside me, kissing my nipples and caressing my abdomen, and when his hands went lower, he inserted his finger in me, and I groaned with pleasure. He removed his clothes and gently parted my legs and entered me. I have never felt anything like his lovemaking. It was slow and tender, ultimately meant to lead me to a climax that would leave me sated and weak. Following this James rested his head in the crook of my neck, held me tight, and let his own passion drain out of him.

"Oh, Alice, I really love you, really, really love you, and have done since I worked with you in the Sudan." We went upstairs to have a shower, but this too ended in bed with a climaxing of power, real sexual power. I had never experienced anything like it. We cuddled together and fell asleep in each other's arms. What an investment that hairdo was! I woke to the sound of gurgling coming from Anna's room and lazily got out of bed, put on a long T-shirt and went through to get her.

"Shall I make a bottle of milk for her, Alice?"

"Just a little please, James—she has a rusk in milk now."

We both seemed to tend to her naturally, thinking as one, and she was soon changed, fed, bathed and dressed. I laid her in her playpen with her toys and mobiles and her favourite musical toy, which played "You Are My Sunshine" over and over.

As luck would have it, Carol arrived to see if I wanted to go out for the day. She followed me into the kitchen and gave me such a nudge I nearly fell over. "What have you been up to, you little devil?" she teased.

"Just what it looks like," I answered smugly. "I don't even feel guilty."

"Why should you? You're a free spirit now, don't forget."

"Yes, I know, but I am still officially married," I reminded her.

James came into the kitchen, and I introduced him to Carol. "James was in the Sudan and is now working at U.C.H.," I said proudly.

"Hello, Carol," he said with a warm smile. "I have to thank you and your husband for all your generosity whilst I was in the clinic in the Sudan. I don't think you realise that you probably saved several lives with your nets and medicines. By the way, where did you get the medicines?"

"If I told you, James, I would have to kill you," laughed Carol. "Anyway, I'll be off and leave you to your own devices, if Anna allows it." Carol kissed me with a squeeze on my arm and let herself out.

When we were alone again and sat at the kitchen table, I said, "What are your plans, James?"

"I would like to spend the weekend with you and Anna if I may."

"I would love that. What shall we have for breakfast? I have a tube of ready to bake croissants that we can have, or scrambled eggs."

James decided that the croissants sounded good, and, in fact, they were. We had them straight from the oven with dripping butter and percolated coffee.

"Have you anything you would particularly like to do with Anna?" he asked me.

"Yes, I would like to go in the open-top tourist bus, as it looks a fairly good day, and I have never done this before."

"We better get cracking then," said James, putting the dishes in the dishwasher. I opened a couple of jars of baby food and heated them and put them in the special flask-like containers made especially for this purpose along with a couple bottles of milk, nappies, wipes and a change of clothes. James and I took no time at all getting ready, and we decided we would buy something for our own lunch. I put on the carrying harness, and James lifted Anna in and fastened the belts and buckles, giving us both a kiss as he did so.

We had a lovely day doing all the tourist things and ended up home shattered.

"I have a lasagne in the fridge that we can have with garlic bread," I said.

"Can I have chips as well?" said James boyishly.

"And you a doctor?" I said, tongue in cheek.

Naturally, Anna had to be dealt with first, and James took charge of the operation with no fuss or bother. Anna was such a good baby, and I must say, especially when James was doing things for her, she always smiled at him.

Anna had a small supper as she had consumed all the food we had taken with us, and by 6.30 p.m., she was sound asleep in her cot.

"Do you want me to get some wine for supper?" James called from the sitting room.

"Not for me, thank you—I think I've broken enough of my vows, but you get some." I said this despite the fact that I felt no guilt about our lovemaking.

"I think I will. I won't be long, sweetheart."

During our meal, I told James about my Open University course.

"That's great," he said, reaching across to hold my hand for a moment. "If you need it, I would be really happy to help. What is your long-term plan?"

"I thought once I get my nursing qualification and Anna is older I could go and work for a charity abroad."

"Still filled with the love of God then," taunted James.

"Always, James, and if, as you say, you love me, you will have to accept that this is my calling. My faith was dented when Carl told me he didn't love me, but I will always have faith and go where I am called."

"I do know, Anna, and I will back you in whatever you choose to do."

It was about 8.30 p.m. when the doorbell rang. I got up to answer the door and was flabbergasted to see Carl standing there. "What do you want?" I asked him coldly.

"I have come to sort out the maintenance payments."

I was cross with his intrusion and just showing up whenever it suited him. "I asked you to do this through my solicitors, and why have you left it so long? I am certainly not going to discuss it now."

Just then, James came into the hall to see what was going on. When Carl saw him, he sneered, "Oh, very cosy. How long has this been going on?"

James spoke before I could. "Actually, it is none of your business if, as you say, anything is going on. You gave up any rights when you left Alice to fend for herself and the baby. So go away, and if you do need to contact Alice, do it through her solicitor as she told you." I could tell that he was getting angrier with every word.

"I want to see Anna," whined Carl.

"Well, you can't, she is asleep, so piss off." James shut the door firmly.

"James, your language, really. I know I am no angel nowadays, but I don't like it when you swear. Thank you anyway for getting rid of Carl. I am grateful."

"I think you will find, my darling, that he has been dumped and is going to try to wheedle his way back into your affections."

"You don't really think that, do you?" The thought of this worried me. "I am still married to him, and I can't deny him access to Anna."

"I know that, but you have got to be prepared, as I suspect he will fight dirty. I never believed in his false image of a God-fearing, genuine man. Don't forget what you told me about him leaving you when you were very young." James took me in his arms and, for the next hour, all thoughts of Carl were eradicated by waves of passion as James made love to me in his tender, wonderful way.

James started his obstetrics and gynaecological six-month posting on 18 July 1970 at U.C.H. He worked really long hours and was on call every other weekend. His prediction of Carl's motives proved right, and I had a letter from his solicitor stating that he wanted unlimited access to Anna. I discussed this with my solicitor, and we agreed that Carl could have Anna for the day once a month. James was not too happy about this, mainly because it meant that I would see Carl on a regular basis, and he knew how seriously I took my wedding vows. He had no need to worry, as I actually disliked Carl intently now having seen the real man.

James would finish his obstetrics and gynaecological posting in January 1971 and would be looking for a post of Registrar in whatever speciality he chose. It looked very much like he would opt for paediatrics. Anna would be nearly one by then, and as James and I lived together as common-law husband and wife, we could easily move anywhere in the country.

Carl had Anna for the first time on Saturday, 24 July 1970. I felt sick the whole day, but he brought her back safe and sound at 6.00 p.m.

"Has she been all right?" I said, taking her from his arms as if snatching her danger.

"Of course. We had a lovely day."

"Did she get on well with Maria?" I taunted him.

"You know full well that I am no longer with Maria." He gave me a measured gaze.

"Are you on your own now then?"

"No, I have a new girlfriend." He was not forthcoming with any more information, and I certainly was not going to show any further interest in his life.

"See you in one month then," I said.

Carl shrugged and said, "I might not be able to make it that day, as we may be going on holiday."

"So much for wanting to see Anna as much as possible!" I snapped.

James was on call at the weekend and had to stay in the hospital. I had arranged to meet up with Carol, Ian, Christopher and Isobel together with Maggie on Sunday, 25 July. We had arranged to meet at the London Zoo, and luckily, the weather was fine and warm. Maggie was full of excitement about going to the Grammar School, and she still took the Sunbeams. "Do you miss your little Corps, Alice?" she asked me.

"I suppose I miss going to the Army, but I really am not worthy, as I live with a man I am not married to, which is looked upon as a sin."

"Stop beating yourself up," Carol interjected. "You have done nothing but good all your life." Carol was such a loyal friend, and I loved her dearly for it.

The day was perfect, Anna was as good as gold, and it was lovely seeing my friends. Maggie asked if we could all go to see her troop get their badges the following Sunday, and we all agreed that we would go—I did say I was not sure if James would come, but I would ask him. I was amazed at how confident and grown up Maggie was even though she was still only eleven years of age.

I lived the nearest to the zoo, so they all came back for supper. Of course, Anna had to be dealt with first, and there were plenty of helpers. Once she had been bathed, fed and snuggled into her babygrow ready for bed, I put her in her playpen, and we started to get a meal ready. We could not make it too late, as Maggie had to get home at an early hour, but Carol and Ian would take her. She was like a second daughter to them too—they were as fond of her as I was. We had a good old pow-wow over our meal and plenty of laughter. Even Anna was smiling, gurgling and dribbling!

After they had all left, I gave Anna a small bottle of milk, and she dropped off before it was finished. I put her to bed and went downstairs to watch a little television. James phoned at 8.00 p.m. and said how much he missed us but that he was really busy. He thought he would be home at about 6.00 p.m. Monday.

"I can't wait to get you into bed," James said huskily.

"Nor I," I replied, and experienced little spasms of pleasure just thinking of him holding me in his arms and making love to me. It seemed to get better and better the more we made love and explored one another's pleasure spots.

Following his call, I made a concerted effort to get on with my Open University work, and the next time I looked at the clock, it was 1.00 a.m. I got up, leaving my papers all over the table, hoping that I would be able to study again tomorrow.

Anna had joined a little nursery at St Andrews Church at the bottom of the road so she would get used to mixing with other little ones. I walked down with her at nine in the morning and came back home with the intent to delve right back into my studies. I didn't have to collect her until one-thirty in the afternoon.

Before I started studying again, I set my alarm so as not to be late collecting her in case I dropped off to sleep. At 10.00 a.m., Carl phoned to ask if he could have her for the rest of the day since this was his last week before the new school year began. I said that would be fine but he would have to collect some things for her and that she must be back home by 7.00 p.m. at the latest. I rushed around and put nappies, wipes, Heinz baby food and a bottle of milk in a knapsack ready for Carl to collect on the way to the nursery. I had hardly finished this when he arrived with a young blonde, whom he introduced as Angela.

I didn't want my daughter spending the day with a woman I didn't know, but I held my tongue on that point. In an effort to dissuade, I said, "It's too early to pick up Anna now. The nursery does not end until twelve noon at the earliest."

Carl was unfazed. "That's fine. We'll just have a walk on Primrose Hill while we wait. See you later then." Carl picked up Anna's knapsack and steered Angela out the door, his arm tight around her tiny waist. I had the distinct feeling that he was showing her off, trying to make me jealous.

James arrived home earlier than expected at 4.00 p.m. "Prof told me to go home because I had such a busy weekend. It was hellish." With that, he pulled me tightly to him, but then noticing the silence, he said, "Where is Anna?"

"With Carl until seven."

"Come on then, let's make hay while the going is good." We ran upstairs and in no time were kissing passionately whilst taking off each other's clothes. "I have missed you so much, Alice."

He caressed me all over until I was pleading with him to enter me. "Oh, James, I love you," I whispered. "Oh, James . . . oh, James. . . ." We climaxed together powerfully.

"Now I am well and truly knackered," said James with a beaming smile.

"Go and have a nice relaxing bath whilst I get supper ready."

"Okay, my beloved Alice, love of my life."

I went down to the kitchen to prepare fillet steak, jersey potatoes and a green salad. I had made a crumble, which I was going to serve with clotted cream so he would not go hungry. I was clearing my work from the table when the doorbell rang. It was Carl, Angela and a grizzling Anna.

"I know it is early, but she has been grizzling all the afternoon."

"Ah, a fair weather parent." I just could not help saying it.

"Actually, I think she's teething," said Angela. "I have two of my own."

I said goodbye, shut the door and cuddled Anna. James came into the kitchen looking pink and gorgeous. "What's up with Anna?" he said.

"Carl's bird thinks she's teething. She certainly is hot and fretful."

"Let me look at her, darling." He took her from me. "I think that's it. I don't think there is anything much going on other than sore gums. We'll give her some Calpol and see how she settles."

"James, what would I do without you? You won't leave me, will you?"

"Alice, I have told you I really do love you and want to be with you now and always."

Anna settled down, and after her bath, lots of cuddles and some warm milk, she fell asleep. "I will take her up, darling," said James taking her from my arms and carrying her upstairs to her nursery. When he came down, he sat next to me on the settee and put his arms around me. "I think we should have an early night too, don't you?" James said with a glint in his beautiful blue eyes.

"Yes, please," I answered shamelessly. Again, we made love, with less passion, but with the same wonderful ending.

Both of us fell fast asleep immediately, and we did not awaken until 7.00 a.m. when Anna made herself heard in no uncertain terms. I picked her up out of her cot and took her downstairs. James got ready for work, and we all sat around the kitchen table having boiled eggs and soldiers.

"I might be a bit late this evening," he said. "We have a long operating list this afternoon." James got up from the table, kissed Anna and then me, long and hard. "To get me through the day without you," he said as he went out the front door.

I got Anna ready and took her to the nursery. When I got back home, I settled down to my studies. Later that day my tutor rang and said she thought I should do a preliminary exam, and if I passed this, I could do some ward work as well. I was delighted and said I would like that very much. The exam was the next Monday, and I really studied hard. When James rang at lunchtime, I told him, and he was thrilled too.

"Who's a clever girl then?" he said, and I could hear the smile in his lovely voice.

"I am!" I boasted.

James was late coming home that evening and was utterly exhausted, too tired to eat his supper. I made him a hot drink, and he went for his shower, peeking in on Anna before he did so.

When he came down and lay on the settee, we discussed how we would manage childcare for Anna when I worked on the wards. We eventually decided that we would get a child minder. James said, "There is a Sister who is retiring, and she might like a top-up to her pension. She is about fifty-six, I think, and very reliable. I am sure she would come here to baby sit rather than your having to do all the running around."

"That would be fantastic. If you ask her and she agrees, we can arrange for her to come and see Anna and the house. Is she married?"

"Widowed," James answered.

"Maggie wants us to go and see her Sunbeam troop get their badges on Sunday, first August. Are you off that day?"

"Yes, the whole weekend, and it will be good to see Maggie, Carol, Ian and the kids."

Sunday came, and we all assembled at my little Corps and watched Maggie bursting with pride as she watched her Sunbeams getting their respective badges from the Corps Officer.

"Do you miss the Army?" James said.

"Yes, very much," I said, holding back the tears.

"I promise you, my darling, when you qualify as a nurse, and there is somewhere relatively safe for Anna that needs our help, we will volunteer."

"Thank you, darling. That would be absolutely wonderful." I smiled at James.

After the badge ceremony was over, we all went back to Carol and Ian's for lunch. "When do you start Grammar School, Maggie?" Ian asked.

"Third September. I can't wait," she said excitedly. After enjoying a delicious lunch accompanied by lots of chatter and laughter, we all did our bit to clear up. James and I said our goodbyes and went home to make the most of his day off! As soon as Anna was asleep, we certainly made the most of being alone together, more than once.

I heard from the Nursing College that I had passed my exam and could start working on wards as an Agency Nurse. Cherry, the Sister whom I spoke about earlier, had agreed to come and act as child minder whenever necessary. My first stint was at U.C.H. at the end of September, where James was working. Every day I learnt more and more on both surgical and medical wards.

Cherry was an absolute gem. Anna loved her, and she cared for Anna as though she were her own.

The months flew by, and we celebrated Anna's first birthday. James had started at Great Ormond Street on a six-month Registrar post at the end of February 1971 and was absolutely run off his feet. I did stints on the Geriatric wards as well as Obstetrics and Gynaecology, and worked as hard as I could to learn as much as possible.

In June we had a lovely party for Anna, as we weren't able to do so in March. We also wanted to surprise all our friends, as we had got married secretly at the Registrar's Office in Hampstead (having got my divorce from Carl of course) with just Anna and Cherry attending, and a couple of James's colleagues as witnesses.

After Anna had torn open her presents and showed off her newly acquired skill at walking, James tapped the side of his coffee cup with a spoon to get everyone's attention. He thanked everyone for coming. As he was speaking, the waiters came around with glasses of champagne and handed them to all the adults.

"I would like to propose a toast to Alice, my beautiful wife, and to my lovely daughter Anna," James said very smugly. All hell let loose.

"Why didn't you tell us?"

"When did you get married?"

"I am so happy for you," said Carol, cuddling me. The rest of the party went like a flash, and it seemed no time when we were home again.

James's posting at Great Ormond Street would finish at the end of August, and we had already volunteered to go to Zambia to help run a school and hospital for the Salvation Army. By the time we had all had the necessary inoculations and packed as much as possible to take with us, we were due to leave. Cherry had agreed to stay in the house during our absence. Carol, of course, was not at all happy about us going and let us know in no uncertain terms. She and Ian came to the airport to see us off on 12 September 1971, and a few tears were shed.

When we arrived at the Mission on 14 September 1971, we were delighted to find a well-equipped and staffed hospital and school. There was a resident general surgeon, Mr Owen Jones, who had retired the previous year; a Mr Gerry Osborne, a retired obstetrician and gynaecologist; and two newly qualified doctors doing their gap year. There were also several trained Zambian nurses who would show me the ropes.

Anna was in her element. Now aged eighteen months, she was walking and talking quite a bit. She was going to attend pre-school classes with the Zambians. The two officers, Major and Mrs O'Brien, were qualified teachers and taught the older children. A Zambian Salvationist taught preschool.

The hospital was quite busy with deliveries, general surgery and medical cases. Contagious patients were in an isolation unit where they were barrier nursed. AIDS was very prevalent in Zambia. James was allocated general surgery whilst I was placed in post-op recovery.

On our first day off, James took Anna and me to the Victoria Falls, which were magnificent. We had a picnic but made a speedy exit when Anna took a keen interest in a snake! Neither of us had any idea what species it was, but we didn't want to take any chances in case it was venomous. We would have to gen up on this sort of thing.

When we got back, I was very sick. This went on most of the night, but I didn't feel ill. It dawned on me that I could be pregnant—I was not sure of the date of my last period.

"James, I think I could be pregnant."

"What? How far along are you?"

"I am not sure—about twelve or thirteen weeks maybe."

"You must see Mr Osborne tomorrow to find out exactly, and you must take care of yourself and our little treasure, my darling. I am so happy," James said beaming.

As soon as we had our breakfast and got Anna to preschool, James marched me over to see Mr Osborne. After he examined me and asked about my general health and previous pregnancy, he stated that he thought I was about fourteen weeks gestation. He arranged the usual blood tests, but the hospital did not have an ultrasound scan.

"Our baby is going to be born in March, perhaps even the same date as Anna," said James excitedly.

Needless to say, Carol was delighted about the new baby and said she would come and stay with us near the expected date to look after me. Maggie sent her love too and said that she was doing well at school.

The hospital was busy continually, and both of us came back to our apartment shattered every evening. Not so Anna, who was now getting into everything, wanting to play, and listen to stories. She loved us to read to her and paid attention throughout the whole story and often asked for it to be read to her again. She was a very good little girl with a sunny disposition, loved her preschool, and was loved by the little Zambian children.

Soon, it was Christmas, and the whole Mission looked festive. Of course, there was no turkey dinner, but we had a lovely carol service with a full house. Two babies were born on Christmas Day, and James had to remove an appendix as well as treat a patient who'd suffered snakebite. All in all, though, we had a good time. Anna had quite a few presents and was very excited about Father Christmas.

My Precious Sunbeam

January was very busy with an outbreak of measles which was very serious for the youngest, some of whom had pneumonia, and, sadly, one little boy died due to complications as he was HIV positive.

February came before we had time to get our breath. All my check-ups were fine, and I was as fit as a fiddle. We were due a couple of days leave, and we planned to do some shopping in Lusaka for the baby, even though I knew Carol would come laden down with gifts.

It was nice having a break, and we did manage to get a few things for the baby and for Anna. On the way home, I had quite a severe pain in my abdomen. "Are you okay, darling?" asked a concerned James.

"I think so," I said, but I wasn't so sure. It was not too long a drive home, but I had another pain before we got there. The pains continued, and James felt my abdomen during one pain and confirmed that I was having contractions.

He went across to the hospital, but Mr Osborne was away until the following evening. The pains were becoming more frequent, and I went to hospital where the midwife examined me and said I was quite advanced in labour and thought it would be a quick birth.

Early in the morning of 18 February 1972, I delivered a 6-pound 8-ounce baby boy, who was beautiful. I held him in my arms and looked with amazement at our little treasure. James then had his turn and wept with joy.

The midwife started gently palpating my abdomen and then asked me to see if the baby would suckle, as the placenta had not delivered. I did so, and immediately had an excruciating pain that made me scream out in agony.

"Alice, what's wrong?" James asked terrified.

"Alice has an inverted uterus and has gone into catastrophic shock and is bleeding heavily," said the midwife. She asked James to get the on-call surgeon.

THE FINAL PART

ALICE

James wasted no time doing what the midwife asked. After the surgeon looked at Alice, he turned to James. "I am so sorry. Alice has gone."

"What do you mean? Let me see her." James took Alice's limp body in his arms. "Alice, Alice, my darling girl, open your eyes!"

"James, it is no good. She suffered catastrophic shock when her uterus inverted, causing a fatal heart attack. There was nothing we could do to save her."

James rocked Alice in his arms, his body wracked with sobs. Major O'Brien came into the room and said a prayer.

"How can you pray to God when Alice has never done anything but good in her life and this has happened to her?" James could hardly say the words through his sobs.

"James, lay her down."

"I will not, and her name's not *her*, it is Alice. Kindly have some respect."

Eventually James lay Alice gently down on the bed and left the room. He phoned Carol, who was too dumbfounded to say anything, and Ian took over the phone. "Do you want us to come and help?

"I presume you will be coming home—"

"As soon as possible," said James. "I would rather you meet me at the airport. I will let you know all the details as soon as possible." As an after-thought, James added, "We have a son."

Everybody rallied and arranged for James, Anna and the baby to fly home together with Alice's body.

Carol and Ian were at the airport to meet James, Anna and the baby, and the funeral directors were there to collect Alice. James sobbed as Carol put her arms around him. Anna looked up at James.

"Where's Mummy?" she asked in a small voice, her bottom lip quivering.

"She had to go away, but she will be watching over you all the time," Ian answered quickly.

Carol said to James, "I thought it best that you all come and stay with us until at least after the funeral so we can look after the children."

"Thank you," said James blankly, at a loss for further words.

"Cherry is looking after the house well," Carol reassured him, "and you will have everything you need when you decide to go home."

Carol took the baby and looked down at him lovingly. "Poor little soul, have you got a name for him yet?" she asked James.

"Yes, Alexander," James answered.

When they arrived at Carol and Ian's, James put baby Alexander in the Moses basket, and dear little Anna stood by him as though watching over him. This set everyone off crying again.

"I have got to pull myself together for Alice's sake," said James. "The children have got to be cared for as normally as possible. Alice told me one time that she wanted her funeral service at her first little Corps, but I'm sure she had no idea we would be making those plans so soon. She was so young . . . only thirty-two." His words caught in his throat. Carl and Ian waited for him to collect himself and continue. "I will get in touch with Brigadier Maloney to see if he will do the service."

The Brigadier was quite devastated by the news, and, of course, he agreed to do the service. He said it would be an honour.

Alice's funeral was conducted on 4 March 1972. Dear Maggie had her Sunbeams form a Guard of Honour as Alice's body was carried in and out of the Army Hall. Cherry looked after the children. Following the service at the crematorium, a meal was provided for everyone who knew and loved Alice throughout her short life.

After the service, James decided that he should go back home to Primrose Hill. Cherry had made a lovely nursery for Alexander and a beautiful little girl's room for Anna. She said she would be delighted to stay on as housekeeper and child minder, as James was going back to work as soon as possible. He had decided that he would specialise in Obstetrics and Gynaecology. He wanted to do everything in his power to prevent such a terrible thing happening to another family.

James never got over the death of Alice. He constantly told the children how much their mother loved them, and he showed them photographs of Alice so that they would never forget her.

James never remarried and eventually became a Consultant Obstetrician and Gynaecologist. Anna and Alexander progressed well at school, Christopher studied Law at Oxford, and Isobel studied Veterinary Surgery, also at Oxford. Dear Maggie went into training to become an Officer in the Salvation Army. Carol and Ian remained a constant help to James.

No one ever forgot Alice, and James still mourns her to this day.

About the Author

Valerie Baxter is a 74-year-old woman who suffers from Dystonia. Her particular symptoms are that she cannot use her favoured right hand and has typed both her books SIGMUND and MY PRECIOUS SUNBEAM with the forefinger of her left hand whilst also coping with the involuntary closure of both her eyes causing difficulty in any continuity of script.

This particular book is based on both truth and fiction.

Review Requested:
If you loved this book, would you please provide a review at Amazon.com?
Thank You